From New York to the Smokies

A Collection of Sam Jenkins Mysteries

Wayne Zurl

Published by

Melange Books, LLC
White Bear Lake, MN 55110
www.melange-books.com

From New York to the Smokies ~ Copyright © 2015 by Wayne Zurl

ISBN: 978-1-68046-078-0 Print

Cover Art by Becca Barnes

The Boat to Prison

Wayne Zurl

Dedication

For the real Kate and Pauly
You've provided fifty years of love and friendship.
Please learn how to drive a stick shift.

The Boat to Prison
Wayne Zurl

Chapter One

I pointed the twenty-six foot Ulrichsen cabin boat southwest from Jones Inlet on Long Island toward the Acid Waters off the New Jersey coast. Driving the heavy lapstreak sea skiff dead into a light breeze on a smooth sea, an occasional swell rose above the ripples, but I steered to compensate, and the hull rolled over the waves effortlessly.

On the rear deck, ten feet behind the open wheelhouse where I sat, my father and his two friends drank beer and talked union business.

Tony Casale, the president of local something-or-other of the Amalgamated Meat Cutters of America said, "That fuckin' Joey Franconero thinks he can get my job next election. Yeah? Fuck him. That's not gonna happen. I know he's screwin' Angelo Saldano's sister. One word from me and Joey's history. You know what I'm sayin', Eddy?"

"Joey's married," my father said. "He's crazy to get involved with Angelo's sister."

I was only seventeen then, July, 1963. But I used to read Newsday, and I remembered that Saldano was a Teamster's labor leader with more than the usual rumored connections to organized crime.

"That's what I'm talkin' about," Casale said and tapped his forehead with the heel of his hand.

"You'd drop a dime on Angelo?" my father asked.

"No, Eddy, I'd let Joey screw me with the membership like he's screwing Rosie Saldano. Yeah, I'd tell Angelo. Whaddaya think? Let Angie catch that prick in the saddle with his little sister, and after that, good-bye Joey."

"Jesus, Tony."

My old man didn't seem used to such drastic or permanent solutions.

I turned for a moment and stared at my father. Worry clouded his usual happy-go-lucky expression. Perhaps he didn't like where the conversation was headed.

He saw me watching him. "Hey, Sam," he said, "give it a little more gas. Let's get there before the fish are all gone."

I pushed the throttle forward slightly. The tachometer showed an extra 500 RPMs, the engine leveled off and sounded a little louder. My father looked a bit more secure with the extra noise.

Casale didn't break five-foot-six in his boat shoes, but he acted like the toughest man alive. He compensated for a small body by having a big mouth and acting like he owned the world. His swarthy good looks and expensive wardrobe may have influenced some people, but his act didn't work on me.

"Timing is everything in an election, Eddy," Casale said. "Look how you made shop steward. I tell Angelo. Angelo *takes care* of Joey when the time is right, and there you go—I run unopposed."

I could still hear their conversation and turned briefly to look toward the rear. My father sat on the engine housing near the stern of the boat, a can of Rheingold beer in his right hand. He shook his head as he listened to Casale's logic. The boat engine purred steadily, and the exhaust gurgled, but I could hear everything they said. They drank enough beer not to think about keeping their voices low.

"I like my job, and I plan to keep it," Casale said, as he drained his own can of beer.

I continued eavesdropping and steered the boat toward New Jersey.

We cleared the jetty back at Jones Inlet an hour earlier. Soon we'd be ready to go after the bluefish.

"Hey, kid, whaddaya figger?" Casale called out. "How much longer till we get inta those blues?"

I looked at my watch. "Half hour, forty minutes maybe, Mr. Casale. You'll start seeing the boats when we get close. We're a little late, but it won't matter. The paper said everybody's killing the blues out here."

"Okay, kid. Give us a heads-up when we get close, ya hear me? And for chrissakes, call me Tony, will ya?"

I flipped the pint-sized creep a two-fingered salute. "Sure, you bet."

A moment later, Casale yelled, "Hey, kid, you want a beer?"

"No, thanks, I'm good." I turned away and looked out the windshield again.

"Nice boy you got there, Eddy. How old is he?"

"He was seventeen in May. He's going into his senior year in September."

"He's a big, good-lookin' boy, almost as big as Rocco here."

"Yeah, he works out. He's strong for a kid. Look at those arms."

I was surprised my father had noticed.

"What's he wanna do after he graduates?"

"I don't know. He's crazy. He's got good grades, but he says he wants to go into the Army. But who the hell knows? If he gets serious with this girl he's got, maybe he'll change his mind. He's nuts about her, so who knows?"

That sounded more like the father I knew.

For the first time, the big man named Rocco spoke. "He'd better not join the Army. Don't he watch the fuckin' news? That place over there, whaddaya call it, Vietnam? Stuff's happenin' over there, ya unnerstand? You mark my words, couple years from now, there's gonna be some shit goin' on, and for what? Huh?"

"Rocco, what the fuck you know?" Tony said.

"Hey, I watch Huntley and Brinkley. I'm just sayin'. Tell the kid ta go ta college, Ed. F.T.A, all the way. Fuck the Army. We all been there. The big war, right? Who needs that shit in some fuckin' hot and sticky jungle?"

Ten minutes later, Tony walked up to the wheel house and stood next to me.

"You hear what we were talkin' about, kid?"

I looked at Casale for a long moment and locked eyes with the little worm. I didn't like him when I met him, and I liked him less after listening to his verbal crap. "No," I said, "the engine noise is too loud. You need something?"

Casale smiled. "Good boy. Your old man says you got a toilet on

3

board."

I pointed toward the open hatchway to the cabin. "Down there, the door on the right."

Casale chuckled. "You're a good kid, Sam, a good kid." He patted me on the shoulder.

"Yeah, thanks," I said, as Casale moved down the companionway. "Pump the handle to flush it, but be sure to close the lid first."

Tony closed the varnished door to the head compartment, and I muttered to myself, "Up yours, you bastard," and entertained the idea of tossing the little weasel overboard.

As we approached the Acid Waters, or the Acid Grounds, as some called it, the color of the water changed from the normal blue-green to a muddy, almost yellow sea. I never knew why people called it acid, but I figured if it was near New Jersey, it had something to do with chemical pollution.

Private vessels, commercial charters and open party boats bobbed on the ocean around the extensive perimeter of the yellow water. I scanned the horizon and spotted a flock of gulls off our starboard bow, hovering over the surface. I pushed the throttle lever forward and aimed the boat for them.

"Hey, Dad," I said. "Get your rods ready. I'm gonna drift over near those gulls. The blues are cutting into a school of bait fish."

As we approached the spot I wanted, we watched more than fifty sea gulls dipping into the water, plucking out half-eaten chunks of spearing and killies. The saw-toothed bluefish had worked themselves into a frenzy, chopping up thousands of bait fish. The water's surface took on a pink tinge from the blood.

"Jesus Christ," Rocco said. "Look at those blues breaking water. They're choppin' the shit outta the little fish."

The three men used stout boat rods, fitted with conventional Penn or Ocean City reels. My father hung strips of cut squid on chrome spoons attached to heavy wire leaders.

"Try and cast 'em as close to the blood as you can get," he told the two Italians. "Don't let the lures go deep. The fish are up top. Stand by. The kid'll cut the engine and drift just outside the school."

At least my old man knew something about salt water fishing.

I snapped a red and white surface plug on the end of my line. My seven-foot, tapered rod held a big Mitchell-Garcia saltwater spinning reel.

After more than an hour of intensive fishing, the birds disappeared. The roiling water smoothed, and the voracious bluefish left for deeper water, sated by their meal of bait fish.

"Whaddaya think, Sam? We finished here?" my father asked. I stood three inches taller and outweighed him by twenty pounds. He looked up slightly when he spoke.

"We could troll deep with jigs or Hopkins lures." I shrugged. "Whatever you want, but the party boats are leaving. I guess so. Anyways, you've got two dozen fish. You want to clean more than that?"

He shook his head. "Okay, start heading back. We'll have lunch on the way."

I turned the ignition key, and the big six cylinder engine kicked in. I pushed the gear lever forward, and the propeller began turning, leaving a small wake. Checking the compass, I spun the spoked wheel hard to the left and waited for a heading of sixty degrees before pushing the throttle forward. The boat surged ahead smoothly until the speedometer read twenty knots. Then I relaxed and settled into the helm seat to get more comfortable.

"Twenty-five fish!" I heard Tony Casale say. "In a little more than an hour. Pretty good, no?"

"Big ones, too, Tony," Rocco added. "Whaddaya figger, Ed? Ten, twelve pounds apiece?"

"Yeah, some even bigger, though. Here's a scale," my father said. "Weigh 'em if you want."

"You see that big one the kid caught? Must be close to twenty pounds," Casale said. "His rod bent like a fuckin' horseshoe. And he caught more than any of us. I gotta get me one of those spinnin' reels."

"They're a pain in the ass," my father said. "You gotta watch you don't tangle the line."

My old man argued with me before and after I bought that rig. I never knew why he disliked spinning reels. Probably a generational thing.

5

"The kid had no problem," Casale said. "Can't be that bad. Hey, Sam, what kinda rod and reel should I get?"

I turned toward the stern and looked at Casale. "Get a seven foot rod from Lon Wanser in Seaford. He makes them right there in his shop. They're expensive, but good. Then go for a Mitchell 302. But a big Penn Spinfisher is okay, too."

Go ahead, I thought, you're a big shot. Spend your money. Go for the best.

"Okay, kid, thanks," he said. "Ya can't argue with success, huh?"

"Yeah," I said. Then I thought, *some people like my father think you're successful, but you're nothing but a little shithead. I should wring your neck.*

After stowing the rods and tackle boxes and adding more water to the fish wells, the men opened the coolers and unwrapped sandwiches.

My father brought me a salami and cheese hero.

From behind us, I heard Tony say, "Hey, kid, you wanna a beer now?"

I looked at my father and raised my eyebrows.

"Sure, why not," he said, "you're bigger than me. You won't get drunk on a can of beer. Gimme one of those Schlitz for the kid, Tony. He found the fish. Let's give him one of the good ones."

For two dozen fish, he should have given me a Lowenbrau.

At 1:30 the wind picked up and blew from the southwest. The following sea pushed the boat toward the barrier beach that sheltered the bays and Long Island from the Atlantic.

I finished my sandwich and sat behind the wheel, sipping a second beer as the Long Beach water tower came into view.

The hum of the engine and the noise of the rolling wake seemed almost soporific. But my senses sharpened when I overheard a conversation more disturbing than before.

Chapter Two

"Hey, Eddy," Casale said, "how about you do me a favor?"

"Sure, Tony, whaddaya need?"

"I was just thinkin'. How about you invite Joey Franconero for a day on your boat?"

"Invite Joey? How can I do that? I've never met him."

"He's supposed to be campaigning at your store this comin' week. Introduce yourself."

"Just like that?"

"Yeah, just like that. Tell him if he wins the election, you want to get more involved in the union. Like you told me. Say you want to go from shop steward to district rep. You understand?"

"You serious?"

"Yeah, I'm serious. You know why?"

"Tell me."

"Cause Joey's stupid. He thinks with his sausage, not his brain. He'll ask Rosie Saldano to come with him."

"You kiddin' me?"

"You ever see Joey's wife? She's a fat Sicilian—with a mustache. Rosie's a piece o' ass. She'll look good in a bathing suit. And Joey's an asshole. He can't resist an opportunity."

"So what'll that do?"

"So I'll drop a dime on Angelo and tell him to meet you at the dock. He finds Joey with the girl. After that—forgettaboutit." Casale laughed and took a cigar from his shirt pocket.

"Just for being out together?"

"You don't know Angelo. He's very protective of his baby sister, and he don't like Joey."

"And what happens with me and Angelo, Tony?" My father's voice reeked with apprehension.

"Don't worry about it. I'll tell him you're working for me. Do this, Eddy, and I'll make sure you get that district rep job." Casale pointed at my father with the cigar to emphasize his point. "There's good money in that job—lots o' fringe benefits. I promise you, Ed. I'll see to it."

"You want me to set up Joey?"

"Did I say that?" Casale laughed and puffed on his cigar. "You hear me say that, Rocco?"

Rocco laughed and tossed a beer can overboard. "No, Tony. I heard you say give Joey a boat ride." He took a Lucky Strike from a soft pack and cupped a Zippo lighter in his hands, trying to shelter his cigarette from the wind.

* * * *

After clearing the second Wantagh Causeway Bridge, I anchored the boat just south of Goose Island where we cleaned the fish.

At 4:30, I took the boat up Alhambra Canal in Massapequa, slowed the engine, spun the wheel all the way right, and approached the dock into the wind. My father hung two fat rubber fenders over the side, walked through the cabin and emerged from the forward hatch.

"Mr. Casale," I called out, "When I come alongside the dock, use the boathook to pick up the stern line. Just hang on to it and I'll fasten it to the cleat after I cut the engine."

"You got it, kid."

From the center of the wide canal, I approached the dock at five miles-per-hour on a forty-five degree angle.

Casale started to look nervous. "Holy shit, kid, you're gonna crash inta the dock. Slow the fuck down."

I smiled, happy to cause the little gangster some agita. And then two feet from the dock, I pulled the gear shift into reverse and gunned the engine. The boat stopped all forward motion.

"Jesus, Mary and Joseph, kid," Casale said. "You scared the shit outta me. Why didn't you tell me what you were doin'?"

I ignored his question, engaged the gears once more and edged up to the dock. My father stepped from the deck onto the bulkhead and wrapped a spring line around the center cleat. The starboard quarter swung toward the bulkhead, and I switched off the engine.

"You got that stern line, Mr. Casale?" I asked.

"Yeah, yeah, wait a minute," he said, as he snatched at the dock line with the boat hook.

* * * *

I watched the fins of Casale's black Cadillac disappear up the gravel drive, unraveled a rubber hose and began washing the boat.

"Why didn't you take any of the fish?" my father asked.

"You think I'd eat something that came out of the Acid Grounds?"

"Everybody eats fish from out there."

I didn't want to argue.

"Mom doesn't like anything but flounder. She says the blues taste too fishy."

"Whatever."

We worked quickly to clean the boat before closing it up and snapping the canvas mooring covers into place.

"Hey, Dad, you aren't going to help that moron set up this Joey guy, are you?"

My father stopped wiping the seat cushions and looked at me.

"Hey, you didn't hear anything, okay?"

"How can I forget if you want me to drive the boat when you take this guy and his bimbo for a swim?"

"I didn't invite you. I can handle this boat as good as you can."

"Bullshit."

"Hey, watch your mouth."

"You're gonna set up a guy to get whacked, and you tell me to watch my mouth. I can't believe this."

"Where do you get this talk? Whacked. For chrissake, you sound like you're on Gang Busters. Tony's a union man, not a mobster."

Even as a teenager, my father's naivety amazed me.

"Sure, Dad, whatever you say. My opinion—those two are a couple of common hoods. Catch a rerun of the Untouchables. It'll be good training."

"What the hell do you know, for chrissake?"

9

"Then ask Pop. He'll tell you."

"Leave your grandfather out of this. I know what I'm doing."

"Pop's been around these union bums longer than you. He wouldn't trust them."

"I told you, forget what you heard. You got pipe dreams."

"Yeah, right. These guys don't hurt people. This is all a fantasy. Like Walt Disney."

Chapter Three

Three days later, at 8 p.m., someone knocked at our front door.

"Sam, see who that is," my mother said.

I looked through the peep hole.

"Two guys in suits," I said and opened the door.

"Don't open that door until you know who they are!"

"It's all right, Ma. I'll take care of it."

I looked at the two men. Both wore dark, three button suits and narrow ties. The older one wore a fedora. The taller, younger one held up a gold badge.

"I'm Detective Scott. This is Detective Brown, district attorney's office. Is Edward Jenkins here?"

"He hasn't lived here in years," I said.

"This is still the address he has on file with the Department of Motor Vehicles."

"I don't know about that. He and my mother have been divorced since '59."

"What's the matter? What's going on here?" my mother asked, standing next to me.

"These are detectives looking for Dad."

"For what?" she asked the policemen, like they worked for her.

My mother, a five-foot-two-inch blonde, didn't let anyone push her around.

"Detective Scott, ma'am." He showed no offense to her attitude. "We want to speak to your husband about some union business. Do you know where we can find him?"

"My ex-husband," she corrected him. "He has an apartment in West Hempstead. I don't have the mailing address. I don't send him Christmas cards. Other than that, no. Try the A&P in Franklin Square. He's the produce manager there."

Brown spoke for the first time. "Not any more, ma'am. He gave up the manager's job when he became a shop steward."

"I didn't know that, but it sounds like him. He liked all that union stuff. Sorry, we can't help you." She turned and disappeared into another room.

"You know your father's address?" Scott asked.

I told them.

"Sorry to bother you, son," Brown said.

The detectives turned and began walking away. I opened the storm door.

"Excuse me," I said to their backs.

Both men turned as I stepped onto the stoop, closing the two doors behind me.

"Yeah?" the older man said. He looked tired and thirty pounds overweight.

The younger man took out a cigarette and lit up.

"My father in some kind of trouble?"

Scott blew out the match and asked, "Should he be?"

"I'm just asking."

Brown said, "Your father is dealing with some genuine bad guys now that he's involved with this union."

"Tony Casale?" I said.

"What do you know about Casale?" Scott asked.

"I've met him."

"And?" Brown asked and pushed the fedora back on his head.

"And he seems like an asshole," I said.

The detectives laughed. Brown took a business card from his pocket and handed it to me.

"Look, son, you hear from your father, tell him to give us a call. It's important." They started walking again.

"Hey, can I ask you another question?"

They turned once more.

"What's that?" Brown said.

"Suppose somebody asked you to arrange to have another guy

someplace at a certain time? And what if you did that, and the guy you made that arrangement with got hurt? Like on purpose. Would you be guilty of something?"

"You're speaking hypothetically now, are you?" Scott said.

His delivery reminded me of Jack Webb on *Dragnet*.

"Yeah, right, hypothetically."

"Well, hypothetically, if you knew or even suspected that the other guy would get hurt, yeah, you'd be an accessory to causing his injuries."

"It's called criminal facilitation," Brown said. "The more the guy gets hurt, the more serious the crimes are."

"And if this guy gets killed?"

"You're in a world of shit, son," Brown said.

I stood there thinking for a moment, nodding my head. An old-fashioned lamppost illuminated the street. I watched a '62 Impala convertible drive by with its radio playing loudly. The Beach Boys wailed out *Surfin' Safari*.

"Okay, thanks," I said, and turned toward the house.

"Hang on, kid." Scott said.

"Yeah?"

"You know something, do you?"

Jack Webb again.

"Maybe."

"If you know about something, now's the time to tell us," Brown said.

"If I do know about something that may happen, and I help you stop it, and maybe while I'm doing this, you can get something on the guy who wanted it to happen, would that count for anything?"

"That's a lot of 'ifs', kid," Scott said.

My mother opened the front door. "Sam, what are you doing out there?"

"Just talking, Ma. I'll be back in a minute."

"It's late. Hurry up."

"Look, I gotta go," I said. "I'll be home tomorrow. If you've got some time, come back in the morning. I'll tell you what I heard."

Chapter Four

My mother left for work at 8:30 the next morning, and I stayed home alone. At 9:35 a white step van pulled up outside our house on Emerson Street.

When the doorbell rang, I answered it. I found Scott and Brown standing there. Scott wore jeans and a striped shirt. He held a tool box. Brown wore a denim shirt hanging outside his baggy pants. I saw Acme Plumbing stenciled on the truck's side, but no phone number. How original, I thought.

A Dugan's Bakery truck stopped across the street. The brakes squealed loud enough for the two detectives to look around. Moments later, the driver carried a basket of bread up the driveway to our neighbor's back door.

Brown turned and spoke first. "Can we come in, son?"

We sat in the living room. Scott asked, "You don't work?"

"I was too late to get a real job this summer. Everything was taken. So I do some clamming. I sell to the Italian grocery stores and restaurants on Hempstead Turnpike. Prices are good this year. I do okay."

"No clams biting today?"

I sighed. "Yeah, funny. I never heard that one before."

Brown laughed. "Give him a break, Jack."

"It's high tide now," I said. "I'll go out later when it slacks and get a couple bushels."

"Okay, son," Brown said, refocusing the conversation, "what do you have for us?"

"If I tell you what I know about Tony Casale, can I get a favor from you?"

"It'll depend what you want, won't it?" Scott said.

"I need help keeping someone from breaking the law," I said.

"Have they done something illegal already?" Brown asked.

"Not yet."

"Easier to stop something from happening than get them out of trouble later."

That answer satisfied me.

For thirty minutes I relayed what I saw and heard on the boat.

"This Rocco you mentioned," Brown said, "was that Rocco Iaconetti?"

"I don't know his last name. He's a big guy, maybe six-two, over two-hundred, dark wavy hair. He looked like Casale's hired muscle."

Scott and Brown smiled at my assessment and nodded to each other.

"Your father agree to do what Casale asked?" Brown said.

"Sounded like he was thinking about it, but he didn't say so."

"That's all very interesting, kid, and we believe you," Scott said. "But there's not much we can do until we know this Joey Franconero gets hurt or killed. Sorry, but that's the way it is."

"This guy Franconero…is he a hood like Casale?" I asked.

"He's new to the union," Scott said. "An up-and-coming guy, but he seems more honest than most. We don't have anything on him yet."

Before the two dicks had arrived, I turned on the kitchen radio. As we sat there, Chubby Checker started singing *Let's Twist Again*. I regretted not turning off the radio before we began talking. That was a good song, but under the circumstances, it sounded juvenile.

"Can't you tap these guys' phones or something and hear what they're planning before it happens?" I asked. "You know, catch them in some kind of conspiracy?"

Brown shook his head and explained. "It's not that easy. We can't just tap someone's phone when we feel like it. We need a warrant. To get a warrant, we'd have to go to a judge and show him reasonable cause to believe someone is in danger or someone is going to commit a crime."

"I just told you what Casale wants to do."

"You're not what's called a reliable confidential informant," Scott said.

"So who or what is?" I asked.

"Someone who's given us proven information before."

15

"That's stupid. How do you start? How do I get proven if I can't start somewhere?"

"Hang on a minute, Jack," Brown said. "Look, son, for you to be our source, we'd have to get a sworn statement from you. You're a juvenile, but you're intelligent. You couldn't remain anonymous unless the judge says so. Because of the people you'd be talking about, that gets sticky."

"I don't understand."

"Look," Scott interrupted. "You'd have to appear before a judge. You tell your story, answer his questions, and if he believes you, we get the warrant."

"Okay, I'll do that. What's the big deal?"

Scott laughed.

"These people are not like the tough kids you meet in high school," Brown said. "They're bad people. That's why we didn't use a police car to come here today. If they found out you gave a statement, they'd... Well, I don't know."

"Yeah, screw them," I said.

Sometimes, when I look back, I think I had more balls than brains.

"You think it's that easy, do you?" Scott said. "Just like us, they have people watching. You come to court and one of their people makes you, you're on their shit list."

I took a moment to consider that.

"How important is it to get this guy Casale?" I asked.

"Very important," Brown said. "He's on *our* shit list."

"Can't you get a judge to meet me somewhere? Someplace they don't have a guy watching?"

The detectives laughed.

"You got some balls, kid," Scott said.

"That's pretty unusual," Brown said. "What have you got in mind?"

"Well, I got the information out on the water. How about having the judge meet me on the water? He could be on a police boat."

Scott looked at Brown. "You know, Dave, that may work. I think we know a judge who'd go for that."

"Why are you so interested in doing this, Sam?" Brown asked. "This is not a game or like a cop show on TV."

"If I do this for you, I want you to give me a chance to keep my father from showing up and taking this guy Joey and the Saldano girl on his boat. I don't want my old man anywhere near those guys if they try to do something to Joey."

"That may be more difficult than you think, kid," Scott said.

Chapter Five

"Hey, Kats, what are you doing tomorrow?" I spoke from the pay phone in a pharmacy at the corner of Uniondale and Jerusalem Avenues.

"It's Thursday, I have earth science. There's a field trip."

"Screw the field trip. I need a partner tomorrow for something special. I'll pick you up at ten o'clock. We'll go clamming."

"Sammy, I can't cut class. I want to get the extra credit."

"It's summer vacation, sweetie. I can't understand why you took a summer school class if you didn't fail something. That's stupid."

"It's not stupid. And why do you need me to go clamming with you?"

"Too much to explain on the phone. I'll run out of change. Trust me. I know what I'm doing. I'll explain tomorrow on the way to the marina."

"You can't tell me now?" Kate Wisniewski asked.

"I need you for appearance sake. And I want you on the boat with me. You're my partner. Come on, this is important."

"Okay, but I don't know why I let you talk me into stuff like this."

"Cause I'm the best looking and most interesting guy you know."

"Oh, pa-leeze!"

"Ten o'clock. I'll tell you all about my adventure on the way to Merrick."

"Okay, I'll be ready."

"Good. Wear that yellow two-piece I like, the skimpy one."

"You're such a pig. But I've got something new you'll like even better."

"Tell me about it."

"It's cut even lower than the yellow suit. And it's got what they call a push-up bra."

"Yikes! I'm getting excited already. What color is it?"

"Red, white, and blue."

"Whoa, patriotic. I can't wait."

The operator cut in and said, "Deposit ten cents for an additional three minutes."

"See you tomorrow." I hung up. A dime was a lot of money; it could buy almost a half gallon of gasoline.

* * * *

I explained the scenario to Kate, got the expected ration of resistance, heard how she thought I was crazy and continued to drive toward Nick's Marina where I docked my boat.

My cunning plan to meet Scott and Brown and an adventuresome judge on one of the county's police boats would take place sometime around noon. I'd spend more than an hour clamming while Kate offered moral support and showed me the new bikini.

From all outward appearances, the Marine Bureau cops would make a routine stop to see my clamming license and check the size of the cherrystones I had harvested. I'd get taken into custody on the patrol boat, supposedly for taking undersized clams, and wait for a summons to be issued.

If anyone was watching, everything would look kosher. But I couldn't imagine why any gangsters would be on the bay. I hoped Scott and Brown didn't use a boat with a plumber's logo on the hull.

Kate stood on the floating dock while I unsnapped the canvas cover on the 1951 Lyman runabout, an old wooden boat my grandfather, the man I was named for, and I rebuilt two years earlier.

A red buoy-shaped float hung on a brass chain attached to the ignition key. I connected the gas line from the tank to the motor, primed the line and turned the key. The thirty-five horsepower Evinrude outboard coughed and caught. Kate wrinkled her nose at the smell, as a little gasoline mixed with the salt water. I checked the engine as it sputtered and discharged water from the exhaust port on the shaft.

I unfastened the two bow lines and watched the sash weights pull the ropes clear of the deck. Kate unwrapped the stern lines and tossed them back on the dock. We always worked well together.

At 10:45, I pushed the gear lever forward and steered the sixteen-foot boat out of the slip at a crawl and into the canal leading seaward.

I stayed in the marked channel as we approached East Bay. South of the point at the foot of Whaleneck Road, I turned east over the mud flats, brought the bow into the wind, and dropped the Danforth anchor. The exposed black mud of a nearby marsh gave the area an extra strong smell that morning.

"They're supposed to show up around noon," I said. "I'll tread for clams here. There's always enough to fill a bushel."

Kate nodded as I pulled off my T-shirt and slipped into the water.

I shivered. "Whoa, the water's chilly."

"I'll stay up here," she said.

"Catch some rays while I dig a few cherrystones. And let's see that new two-piece you bought."

Kate took off a pair of Bermuda shorts and unbuttoned her sleeveless blouse. She dropped the blouse on the rear seat and said, "Ta-da," modeling her new swim suit.

"Holy mamma!" I said. "This water may be cold, but I'm getting an appropriate reaction."

"You can be so disgusting when you want to."

"You wouldn't have bought that unless you wanted me to like it."

"I guess." She smiled and wrinkled her nose again.

"You look like a movie star, sweetie. Those drawers are three inches below your belly button."

"They are not drawers, Samuel."

"Whatever."

"So you like it?"

"Of course I like it. That push-up bra is the best thing I've seen since Jaguar came out with the XK-E."

I reached up, trying to grab her hand.

She moved a few inches away. "I'm not letting you pull me into that cold water, buddy boy. Hey, aren't you supposed to be clamming?"

"Okay. Put on the radio. It's in my duffle bag."

Kate dialed in WABC. Herb Oscar Anderson said, "Here's Gogi Grant with her 1956 hit, *The Wayward Wind.*"

"Kats, you look beautiful." I dropped two chowder clams over the gunnel and into one of the baskets sitting on the deck.

The breeze blew her dark brown hair around slightly. I loved that tousled look.

"Thank you," she said. "I'm glad you like the new suit."

I smiled and looked into her big brown eyes before dropping my right shoulder back into the water to retrieve another clam. "I like *you*. You make the suit look great. You could be rich and famous if you let me send your picture to *Playboy*."

"Dig your clams, buster, and forget about *Playboy*." She reached out over the boat and ran a hand through my hair.

"You're such a prude," I said and dropped two small cherrystone clams into a different bushel. "Wanna go skinny dipping tonight?"

"I thought you're getting arrested today." She showed me a million-dollar smile. "What would happen if I didn't bail you out?"

A pair of terns flew low over the boat, screeched, and disappeared toward the land.

"Besides hating you for the rest of my life," I said, "nothing. It's all an act. I'll never leave the police boat. And I'll be on the lam this afternoon, just like James Cagney in *White Heat*." Another chowder clam went into the basket before I grinned and said, "You doity rat, the coppers will never take me alive."

Kate shook her head, and Connie Francis began singing *Where the Boys Are* as a thirty-six foot, police cabin cruiser rounded the point south of Wantagh State Park.

"Okay, Cody Jarrett, your friends are coming," Kate said.

She bent over the gunnel, her face only a few inches from mine. I kissed her and looked down at her generous cleavage.

"If you stay bent over like that, sweetie, I'll forget what I want to tell these guys."

"You are such an idiot," she said and blushed a little.

"You'd better put your blouse on. The judge may be an old guy with a weak heart."

"Oh, shut up."

The judge turned out to be a good-looking forty-four-year-old ex-ADA named Paul Crenshaw. Kate sat in a deck chair outside the wheelhouse of the police Egg Harbor cabin cruiser, while the two detectives and the judge questioned me. Two of the three uniformed officers assigned to the patrol boat puttered around on deck. The third, a sergeant, stayed in the cabin.

After I signed my statement, Scott affixed his notary's stamp on the page bottom and countersigned the document.

"You understand that any false statements made here would constitute a class A misdemeanor?" Scott asked.

"I didn't know that, but everything I told you is true," I said.

The judge broke a hint of a smile. "Sam, you know that your father may be complicit in a conspiracy to commit a serious crime?"

"Yes, sir, but these two officers told me that if I gave you this statement, they could get a warrant to tap Tony Casale's phones. If they overhear him setting up this guy Joey Franconero and if I can keep my father away from his boat on that day, you'll forget about him."

"They explained that to me. While I don't like letting a guilty person go unpunished, I've seen worse things done in the name of justice."

"I don't want to see my father go to jail for doing something stupid. He's not a criminal. But I don't see any reason why Detective Scott can't scare the hell out of him after this is over."

Everyone in the cabin laughed.

"How do you plan on keeping him from going to his boat?" Crenshaw asked.

"I'm working on that, Your Honor."

Chapter Six

At 7 p.m. Thursday, I sat in the living room reading a copy of *Rabble in Arms*. The wall phone in the kitchen rang.

"Sam, it's your father," my mother said.

I walked into the kitchen and picked up the receiver as my mother left the room.

"Yeah, Dad, what's up?"

"Is the boat gassed up?"

"Your boat?"

"Yeah, whaddaya think?"

"Well, my boat is gassed and ready to go, but we didn't stop at the gas dock when we brought your friends in, did we?"

"Do me a favor, smart-ass? If you've got nothing to do tomorrow, drive down and top off the tank. I'll give you the money on Sunday. Okay?"

"I don't know if I can get a car tomorrow. If I can, I was going to go clamming. I haven't got much cash right now."

"Haven't you sold any clams lately?"

"Not lately."

"Jeez, I need the boat to be ready for Saturday morning."

"What's going on?"

"I'm taking somebody out for the day. It doesn't look good stopping for gas first thing. Looks like I'm hinting for the guy to pay for the gas."

"Yeah, can't let one of those union Guinzos spend money."

"Don't get smart."

"Who's going? Tony and his stupid friend?"

"No, another guy."

"An important guy?"

23

"Yeah, an important guy."

"Okay, I'll see if I can get a ride. I'll ask Pauly Greco. If you loaned me money to buy a car, I'd be able to do stuff like this for you."

"Save the money you make, and don't piss it away on pizza. Then you can buy your own car."

"Yeah, spoken like a true Scotsman."

"Don't get wise."

"I'll try my best." I wanted to elicit a specific answer from my father so I tried leading him a little. "But if I can't get a ride, I'll call you. Then you can call this guy. Maybe you'll have to tell him to come later or cancel if you don't want him with you while you gas up."

"I can't cancel, and I don't have his phone number."

It worked. I smiled to myself.

"I'll try to get there and gas the boat for you," I said, "but if I can't, just go there early. It'll take you what, a half hour to go to the pumps and get back to the dock?"

"Try your best. This is important."

"Okay, I'll work on it. I'll let you know."

"Good."

"You coming here on Sunday?" I asked.

"Yeah, you wanna go fishing?"

"Sure. Let's stay in the bay. We'll catch a million blowfish. Okay if I bring Kate?"

"Yeah, I'll see you around nine."

"Okay, see ya."

Ten minutes later, I called the District Attorney's Rackets Bureau. After a transfer, I got connected to Detective Scott.

"I just got a call from my father. Sounds like Saturday's the day."

"That's what we think. Yesterday's taps sounded good. Your call this morning should show up, too."

"You got my mother's phone tapped?"

"Your father's."

"Jeez, like that book with Big Brother watching."

"Yeah, something like that."

"He wants me to gas his boat, only I don't have that much cash."

"You need money, do you?"

"It would look funny if I said I'd gas the boat and then I didn't."

"How much you need?"

"We went out all the way to Jersey with Casale and Rocco. I don't know, at least twenty dollars, maybe more." Even marine gas was cheap then.

The line went silent for a long moment.

"So, you want me to give you some cash?" Scott asked.

"Yeah, that'll help me. Don't worry. I'll pay you back next week."

"Alright, don't you worry about it. I'll meet you tomorrow. You're going to Massapequa, are you?"

I started to think Jack Webb was getting an attitude.

"Yeah, in the morning."

"I'll be in the parking lot of the Farmer's Market on Merrick Road about 9:30."

"Okay, I'll drive my mother to work and then meet you. I'll be in a blue and white Chevy."

* * * *

On Friday night, Kate and I sat in a booth at Borrelli's Restaurant on Hempstead Turnpike, across from Salisbury Park. The juke box started playing *Blueberry Hill* by Fats Domino. We were each eating a slice of pizza and two more lay on a tray in the middle of the table.

"I think you're crazy to do this," she said. "What if you get caught?"

"What if *we* get caught? I need a helper or two."

"You want me to go with you?"

"Yeah, it'll be easy. And I'll keep my moron father from going to jail."

"You hope."

"Don't worry, I will. Piece of cake. I asked Pauly to come, too."

"Great. The blind leading the blind."

"Pauly's a good guy."

"I know that. He's just not much of a James Bond."

"What do you know about James Bond?"

"We saw *Dr. No*," she said.

"Wonderful. Now you're a trained professional."

* * * *

Later that night, Kate and I stopped in front of a small Cape Cod on Alcyon Place. I beeped the horn twice. Paul Greco opened the front door and trotted down the walk. He opened the back door of the '53 Bellaire and jumped in.

"Top o' the mornin' to ya," he said.

"Look outside, Spiff. It's after10:30," I said.

"Figure of speech. Where you been all your life?"

Pauly was almost as tall as me, a little heavier, and had short dark hair.

"You bring your hunting knife?" I asked.

"How many Italians you know who don't carry a shiv?"

"You've got a point. You ready?"

"I was born ready. Where we goin'?"

"West Hempstead."

"Almost another planet."

I put the car into first gear and started driving. Twenty minutes later, I pulled up a few doors away from the two-family home where my father rented the upstairs apartment.

"There are still lights on downstairs," Kate said. "You're going to get caught."

"You may look like a James Bond girl, but don't quit school and join the CIA. You have no faith. Relax. We'll wait till 11:15. Everybody goes to bed after Tex Antoine and Uncle Weatherbee."

"Unless they watch the Tonight Show," Pauly said.

"You're an encouraging bastard."

"Just the facts, Chief," Pauly said.

"What happens if someone catches you?" Kate sounded worried.

"Jeez, I should have come alone."

"I'm right behind you, Chief. Whaddaya want me to do?"

"I need a wheelman. I'm going to cut the four valve stems on my father's car, the brown and white '59 Galaxy parked over there." I pointed across the street. "With four flats, he won't be able to go anywhere tomorrow morning."

"Sounds about right," Pauly said.

"I'll get out here," I explained, "walk over and do the street-side tires first. When I go around to the curbside, you drive up and open the back door. I'll jump in. You drive away. Simple, huh?"

"Not so simple, Chief."

"What now?"

"I can't drive stick."

"Oh, for chrissake."

"Sorry," he said.

"Okay, Kats, you're the wheelman."

"Sammy, you showed me how to get the car rolling in first gear. In the driveway. I'm not much good driving a standard shift."

"You're our only hope."

"Oh, man, we have to rely on the Polish princess?" Pauly said.

"You, shut up," Kate said.

"Okay, kiddo, do your best," I said.

We waited an extra five minutes after the lights went off in the house. Then I flipped the switch on the dome light so it wouldn't illuminate the car's interior when I opened the door. Pauly handed me a Case hunting knife.

"Is it sharp?"

"Like a razor."

"You're a real pro, Spiff."

"Like Avis, I try harder."

"Okay, Kats, when I get out, slide over. Start the car when you see me crouch down in the road. When I go to cut the last two valves, drive up just past the Ford. Remember, no lights."

"Oh, Sammy, why do I do these things for you?"

"Cause I'm slicker than James Bond."

"Oh, pa-leeze."

"Whenever Bond does something like this, he gets captured by the bad guys."

"That's what happens in fiction, sweetie. It's sort of a rule writers have."

"It's a stupid rule. If he was good at his job, he wouldn't get caught."

"I read a book once," Pauly said.

"Once?" Kate said.

"Yeah. I'll finish it someday, I guess."

"Enough chatter. Let's go," I said.

I walked quietly to my father's car. Luckily, no porch lights were on, and the closest lamppost stood almost a hundred feet away.

I crouched down, looked up and down the street and slowly cut the first valve. A muffled whoosh sounded in the night air. No one seemed to take notice. I cut the second valve stem and heard the same subdued whoosh. So far, so good.

I checked the street again and circled around the front of the car to the grass strip alongside the curb. Kate put the Chevy in gear and edged down the road, rolling a few feet past the Ford's rear fender. I sliced the third stem too quickly and heard a loud, quick escape of compressed air. Nearby, a dog barked—once, twice, three times. I duck-walked to the fourth wheel. A porch light flicked on next door. The dog continued to bark. I cut the last valve and sprinted toward the open door of the Chevy, tossing the knife into the wheel well and whispering, "Go, go, go!"

Kate let the clutch out too fast and stomped on the gas. The ten-year-old Chevy lurched forward, kicked three times, and finally smoothed out as a second porch light came on.

Two hundred yards up the street, I said, "Shift into second."

Kate said, "How do I do that?"

The engine whined, but only accelerated slightly.

"Step on the clutch and push the stick up."

"Which one's the clutch, again?"

"Oh, jeez!"

"Don't yell. I'm trying."

The Chevy moved forward at twenty-five miles an hour, sounding more like a hundred.

I looked at Pauly. "This is your fault, Spiff."

"Don't look at me, Chief. I'm just the guy with the knife."

I leaned over the seatback and grabbed the column shifter.

"Step on the left pedal."

She did, and the engine revved higher. I pushed the lever into neutral.

"Take your foot off the gas, hit the brakes and slide over. I'll drive."

* * * *

28

A half hour later, I stopped the car in front of Paul Greco's house.

"As far as anyone's concerned, we stopped at Dave Shor's to get hamburgers. No one remembers who comes into a drive-in," I said.

"You got it, Chief. You lie, and I'll swear to it," Pauly said.

"Spoken like a true Italian. Thanks, I'll see ya."

I drove two blocks and turned off Front Street into Kate's driveway.

"Why does he call you Chief?" she asked.

"I told him my Great Uncle Harry was a Mohawk. Pauly doesn't remember he's only related by marriage. He thinks I'm an Indian."

"Really?"

"Who knows? That's Pauly."

"Why do you call him Spiff?"

"I heard his uncle talking about the clothes Pauly wears when he dresses up. You've seen his shiny suits and colored shirts. The uncle called him a spiff, like in spiffy dresser. I never heard the term before, but I think it fits."

Kate nodded. "I better go in before they lock me out."

"Okay. I'll pick you up tomorrow. And thanks for the help."

"I wasn't much help."

"Sure you were. You added moral support."

"Of course I did."

"And you belong with me."

"Night." She smiled and gave me a long kiss.

"Wow," I said and kissed her back.

"Do you love me?" she asked.

"Of course. I wouldn't kiss someone I didn't love."

"I don't believe that."

I smiled. "Doesn't matter. Believe what you want. I'm still going to marry you some day."

"Are you going to ask me first?"

"I just did."

"Not really."

"Don't be so formal. You'd love to marry me. I'm a good catch."

"Says who?"

"All the girls."

"Name them."

"I'll need my little black book."

"Yeah, right."

I kissed her again.

"See you tomorrow?" I asked.

"Of course."

Kate went in, and I began the short drive home. As I pulled out onto Front Street, I turned on the radio. A commercial for Wild Root Cream Oil ended and Phil Phillips began singing *The Sea of Love*. I listened to the words and knew the feeling.

* * * *

The next morning I called the DA's office.

"Hello, is Detective Scott or Detective Brown there?"

"They're out on a case. Can I help you?"

"What did you say your name was?" I asked.

"Sergeant Dunn. Who's this?"

"Scott said I could talk to you. I did something for the detectives last night. I just wanted to tell them it worked out.

"Is your name Sam?"

"Yeah, right."

"They're in Massapequa now. They plan on making an arrest shortly. Is everything cool with you?"

"It is. I doubt my...ah, the other person will get anywhere for hours. So, are we square?"

"As far as I know. I'll have Scott or Brown call you."

"I won't be home. I'll call them. What time?"

"This afternoon, before five."

"Okay, thanks."

* * * *

That night, Kate, Pauly and I sat in a booth at Borelli's.

I said, "I wish Mrs. Borelli didn't know we went to school with her son. I look old enough to pass for twenty-one, and I'd like a glass of wine with my eggplant parmigiana."

"I wouldn't mind a nice-a bottle o' Dago red myself," Pauly said.

Kate made a face, shook her head and asked, "Is your father off the hook?"

She acted like a goody-two-shoes in those days, but if I had the wine, she'd drink her share.

"Yeah, I spoke to Brown this afternoon. He said they recorded a call from Tony Casale to Angelo Saldano. Casale told him where to find Joey Franconero and his sister at the canal. Saldano said he'd *take care* of Joey. Six cops were waiting at the dock before lover boy got there with his girlfriend. Scott found two Guidos who worked for Saldano parked near my father's boat. When they searched the car, Brown found two unregistered guns. I don't know what they'll make stick, but my old man never showed up, and he seems okay for now. Brown explained how the law works. He said something about an incomplete overt act on my old man's part. Beats me, but I trust him."

"And nobody knows you're involved?" Kate said.

"They're going to pick up Casale, that guy Rocco, and my father at the labor lyceum on Monday. After the cops question them, they'll let Rocco and my father go. Casale stays. Sounds like it'll work."

"Does your father know you flattened his tires?" Pauly asked.

"What tires?" I asked. "I don't know what you're talking about. Kats, you know something about tires?"

"I don't know anything about no tires, Sammy."

Kate and I laughed at her answer. Pauly looked confused.

After a brief moment he said, "Hey, Chief, I think you liked playing with those detectives. Ever think about getting a job on the cops?"

I shook my head. "Never crossed my mind. They don't make much money, but who knows, maybe someday they will. I'd like to go into the Army. Ever hear about this new group JFK started? They call it Special Forces."

Pauly shook his head, and Kate frowned.

"They're like that bunch from World War Two, the guys who parachuted behind emery lines and organized a resistance. That actor Sterling Hayden did it in Yugoslavia. That sounds interesting to me."

"And what am I supposed to do while you're off being a soldier?" Kate asked.

"No problem. You come with me."

Her frown came back. "Yeah, sure. Pauly's right. You should think about being a policeman."

"You bet, sweetie. I'll think about it."
I smiled, but kicked Pauly in the shin.

* * * *

After my five years in the Army and sixteen in the reserves, twenty with the police in New York and now as chief of police in beautiful downtown Prospect, Tennessee, I think about my old cases often. It's been a long time since I slashed my old man's tires, but in spite of all the history, a guy never forgets his first brush with the law, even if it's on the good guy's side.

THE END

Favors

Wayne Zurl

Dedication

To all the former members of Command 5212

Favors
Wayne Zurl

June 16th, 1985. Long Island, New York

Elizabeth Carmella Lopez-Cruz worked as a police community service aide. If Liz tired of that job, she could enter a beauty pageant and make it through a few rounds based on looks alone. Once Liz engaged in conversation, it became evident she possessed the personality of an eel.

In addition to being beautiful, Ms. Lopez-Cruz was of Hispanic origin and bi-lingual. The last two factors qualified her for the CSA job.

Liz worked in my office. We didn't actually need a community service aide, but the program was famous for placing those young people in less than useful positions.

At 2:15, I looked out my office door and watched her storm into the squad room. Liz stopped at her desk and pulled a large purse from the bottom drawer. She whispered something to Nancy, my secretary, and nearly flew into the hallway.

Three detectives sat at their desks. They all looked up at Nancy, at each other, and then all four turned and looked back at me. I shrugged.

"What was that all about?" Fred Mazzio asked of no one in particular.

"She told me she needed half a sick day," Nancy said, and tossed a pair of reading glasses on her blotter.

I stood and moved to my doorway.

"She told me she had her polygraph appointment at one o'clock," Mike Rodriguez added. "You think Artie asked too many questions about her sex life?"

"Mandel is no idiot," Mazzio said. "He wouldn't say anything to get himself jammed up. Who knows? Our Lizzie is a bit strange."

"She say anything else, Nance?" I asked.

"No, Sam. She just said, 'I don't feel well. Put me in for half a sick day.'"

"Thank you, Mizz Walnicki. No one else in the building has a secretary who can give verbatim accounts. I'm impressed."

She smiled.

"Yeah, and she's got a great body," Fred mentioned.

"Careful, Freddie, that's sexual harassment," John Gallagher said. "Nancy might get your ass tossed in the slammer." Gallagher took a moment to laugh at what he thought was funny. "You'd look good wearing stripes."

"Frederick, apologize to Nancy," I said. "Gallagher, shut up, and get back to work. This conversation is going downhill. I'll call Mandel and see if he caused Lizzie's snit."

I tapped four digits into my phone and waited for someone to answer in the Polygraph Unit. On the sixth ring someone picked up.

"Hello, Polygraph."

The voice didn't sound familiar.

"Who's this?" I asked.

"Detective Mazurki… Who's this?"

"What are you doing in Polygraph, Gus? Things not busy in the chief's office?"

"I know that voice. Lieutenant Jenkins?"

"Yeah, I'm looking for Artie Mandel."

"He's not here. I was just walkin' by and heard the phone. Maybe he's in the men's room."

"Do me a favor, and leave him a note to call me at extension 2462."

"Sure, 2-4-6-2, you got it."

"Thanks, Gus—and give the chief of detectives a kiss for me."

"Yeah, right, he'll love that."

I hung up as Detective Arthur Mandel walked into my office holding a few sheets of paper.

Artie was tall, balding and appropriately overweight for a guy who spent his working life behind the wheel of a lie detector. I thought he looked more like a podiatrist in his brown three-piece suit.

"Doctor Mandelbaum, I was just looking for you," I said.

"Oh?"

"Sit down. Let's talk about Liz Lopez."

"That's why I'm here."

"Did you two have a falling out?"

"Not because of anything I did. But you've got one strange young lady there."

"How so?"

"As you know, Frankie O'Brien is doing an update background investigation on her. She passed the last PO's test, and she's eligible for promotion."

I nodded. Those were things I knew.

"I was the lucky guy to get her polygraph appointment."

"So what set her off? She came down here, crashing around like a bull in a china shop and then banged in for half a day."

"Right from the get-go I knew she'd be a problem. Besides being a drip, she's nervous as hell."

"Maybe she's got white coat syndrome. You do look like a doctor, you know."

"Will you stop with the doctor shit already?"

"Why do you make her nervous?"

"Yeah, right, it's me. Anyways, I did a standard pre-test interview. With that, she was good because she only gave one word answers. I couldn't get confused."

"You're being caustic, Arthur."

He let my observation go unanswered.

"When we finished with that, I took her into the machine room. I didn't even stretch the cord around her chest. I left the door open and let her do it herself. Then I hooked up her fingers, showed her the card trick so she believed in the machine, and then I asked her my standard six questions."

He stopped to look at me through the tops of his bi-focals. As he continued to speak he glanced at his report.

"She had a lousy base-line, but it looked consistent enough. Her pulse was constantly high, a hundred-and-twenty. When I asked her the catch-all question, the one about has she lied to me even once during the test or pre-test, she said no. She bombed that—big-time.

"Then I did something I usually don't do. I told her to relax, and I went outside for a minute. I let her settle down before I came back and asked her the same question again. Same results. She's a definite untruthful."

"Did you ask her anything more?"

"Of course, but not on the machine. I unhooked her, took her back to the interview room and told her about the results. She started getting huffy, told me she didn't lie. Sounded insulted. I gave her the standard spiel—you know, tell me now, all's forgiven, blah, blah, blah.

"The nicer I was, the more upset she looked. I gave up. She wouldn't go for spit."

"Any ideas based on her body language during the pre-test?" I asked.

"Nothing. She was nervous and jerky when I asked her if she had any hobbies. She was uptight over everything."

He shook his head and looked annoyed.

"Look, Sam, I'm gonna give the report to Frankie, but since you're her boss, I thought you'd want to know."

"Thanks. I always love to have my afternoons ruined."

* * * *

At ten-to-nine the next morning, I made a stop at the coffee maker in the Juvenile Section next door. I said hello to the duty sergeant and the deskman and then wandered into my office.

I heard a broken chorus of "Mornin', boss", "Hey, boss-man" and "Sambo, nice of you to join us," from two detectives and my executive officer, Sergeant Joe Dolinski.

Nancy's desk was empty. The woman's never late, but she's never early.

Liz Lopez sat at her desk, head down, reading something on departmental stationery. She tapped the eraser end of a long pencil on her blotter to a tune unheard by anyone else in the room.

I set my coffee down, took off my sport jacket and sat behind my desk. I dialed Liz's extension.

She answered on the first ring.

"Lizzie, it's Sam. Come back here for a minute."

She looked back toward my doorway. Our eyes met.

"Right now?" She sounded like I interrupted her in the middle of neurosurgery.

No, tomorrow, after lunch.

"Yeah, please."

"Yes, sir."

Liz walked in and sat in one of the guest chairs and waited for me to speak.

When I first met Liz, I wondered why she wanted the CSA job. It was no secret that many of the female CSAs wanted to marry good-looking cops. Then I got to know her. Liz seemed interested in being a cop, but she reminded me of our cat, who had been taken away from her mother too soon. The cat never learned the social graces of her species and neither had Lizzie. Toss in terminal moodiness and there you are. However, she was a competent clerical worker and part of my professional family.

She waited, staring at me. Not even a hello.

The only person close enough to my office to hear what I wanted to discuss with Liz was Mike Rodriguez. His desk abutted the wall next to my doorway. I didn't think what Liz may tell me was anyone else's business.

"Mikey, you got a minute?" I yelled.

"Yeah, boss, whaddaya need?"

He stood up and looked into my office, his right hand resting on the butt of a nickel-plated Detective Special he wore on his right hip. His sleeves were rolled up, and at 9 a.m. his tie was already undone. I tossed him my key ring.

"Do me a favor and gas my car."

He looked at me like I had two heads.

"Since when do I gas your car?"

I looked back at him silently. Liz looked at him and then at me. Mike stood there.

"Go gas his car, you Pol-a-Rican idiot," Fred Mazzio said.

"Huh?" Mike said. Then a light bulb went off somewhere in the recesses of his mind. "Oh, okay, boss, sure, right away."

Then he disappeared.

Liz spoke for the first time. "What's Pol-a-Rican mean?"

"Mike is half Polish and half Puerto Rican. The guys kid him."

"I don't know if I like that."

"It's all in fun. You know how cops are. He doesn't mind."

That seemed to satisfy her—or not. Her expression rarely changed.

"Feeling better today?" I asked.

"I guess." Her long, dark hair looked just wavy enough. It fell two inches below her shoulders. I knew women who would kill for hair like that.

"Did something happen during your polygraph test that you want to talk about?"

"I don't think so."

Mandel was right. Liz seemed like a classic case of flat affect. No expression. No inflection. No passion about anything. It looked like she was just putting in her time on earth, waiting for the end.

"Detective Mandel told me you had problems with the test. He's going to put that in his report to Investigator O'Brien. I'd like to give you a chance to tell me…whatever you need to tell me."

"Sorry, I don't know what to say, Lieutenant. I took the test, and then I didn't feel good. I needed to go home."

"Did Mandel do or say anything you found objectionable?"

"No."

"Did you withhold something that bothered you?"

"No."

"Did you tell a lie? Even a small one?"

"No."

"You know if O'Brien finds something in your background that you lied about, you could be denied the promotion to police officer?"

"I know."

And it looked like she didn't care.

"Liz, sometimes candidates think unimportant things are more meaningful than we do. In a case like that, the lie about what you did is more important than the act itself. You understand?"

"Yes."

"You're tough to get through to, Lizzie."

She shrugged, sat there, her hands in her lap, her shoulders hunched forward.

"You haven't done any drugs since we hired you, have you?

"No."

"Even a little grass? Maybe just took one hit at a party? Something that would be in the back of your mind and make the polygraph waver?"

"No. I've never done drugs."

"Okay," I said. "Thanks for your time."

She stood up, did a right-face and walked out of my office. *Miss Personality.*

* * * *

I finished my coffee, initialed a dozen completed cases and stood up. It was ten o'clock. I put on my jacket and walked into the main office.

"Joey, get your coat. Saddle up, we're going on the road. I've got some police work to do."

"The game's afoot, huh, Sam? You don't want one of us to be here in case the bosses call down looking for us to do something?"

"Screw them." I heard a few snickers from the guys in the squad room. "I can't wait around for them to call and say they need someone to wipe their noses. Come on, we've got things to do."

Nancy said, "Oh, boss, I love it when you talk tough like that."

"Thank you, I'm glad somebody does. Come on, Joey, I'll drive."

Dolinski grabbed his powder blue blazer. It complimented his silver-gray hair. He looked like he just stepped off a page of the Sears' catalog.

From the side door of headquarters, my unmarked Plymouth sat a hundred yards into the parking lot.

It was mid-June, and the Long Island weather seemed ideal. Under a clear blue sky, the deciduous trees were in full leaf. Birds sang a variety of songs as they flew from tree to tree around the parking lot. Wild flowers grew on the roadsides waiting to be cut down by the highway crews.

I opened the driver's door of my Fury and tossed the keys across the roof so Dolinski could open his side. We settled into a car warmed by the morning sun.

"Where we going?" he asked.

"North Bellport."

"Jeez, Sam, I haven't had shots lately."

"It's not that bad, Joey. Stick with me, we'll live."

"You used to work there. Why do you want to go back?"

"I want to see Lizzie's father."

"Liz lives there?"

"Yeah, I remember her when she was just a kid. Her old man's a first-class shitbag, but I need to run something by him."

"Like what?"

"You hear what Mandel said about her poly test?"

"Just some bullshit from the guys. What's to know? Everybody lies about something. Let Frankie O'Brien iron it out."

Joe was a cynic.

"I don't know what's wrong. She's not saying anything, but there's something there. I've got this feeling. Something besides puberty gave her that pain-in-the-ass personality."

"And you'd like to work in Applicant Investigations now?"

"Have you got anything better to do today?"

"I'm right behind you, boss."

Joey knows when it's best to go with the flow.

I turned south off the Sunrise Highway onto Station Road. The neighborhood got more undesirable with every hundred yards. In a few minutes, I turned left on Brookhaven Avenue and then right onto the six-hundred block of Bellport Avenue.

Liz lived at number 632. It was one of the few two-story homes in the neighborhood. The Prussian blue paint on the shingles peeled like a week-old sunburn. Someone may have considered the scattered foundation shrubbery landscaping, but I didn't. At least it gave the wandering dogs somewhere to lift their legs. The lawn, such as it was, consisted of half weeds, half dirt and a liberal scattering of supermarket circulars, fast-food wrappers and night deposits from the local mutts.

A moth-eaten easy chair sat on the ten-foot porch that stretched in front of the entrance. A pock-marked '72 Nova was parked in the driveway with the hood up. A pair of dark blue pants stood next to the left fender. The upper half of the attached body was folded over the engine compartment.

"Just so you don't look stupid when you see Hector Lopez," I said, "expect the worst-looking guy on earth, a real unfortunate."

"That's all you're gonna say?"

"Besides being obnoxious, he's disfigured, a burn victim. He looks like Mister Potato Head. Don't be surprised."

"Jesus H. Christ, why do you do these things to me, Sam? I was minding my own business, getting ready to make a few bets at OTB, and you bring me into the heart of darkest Bellport."

"You're safe with me, kiddo. They still think I'm the mayor here."

We got out of the Plymouth and walked up the short driveway.

"Excuse me," I said to the blue pants.

Joe looked around. He didn't seem happy with our surroundings.

No response from the owner of the trousers. I looked at Joe. He shrugged.

"Mr. Lopez?" I upped my volume.

Still nothing.

"Christ almighty!" I lost patience.

Joe smiled. I took a handful of pants belt and tugged.

"Hey, what the hell? Whadda jou doin', man?"

Hector Lopez arose from under the hood and turned to look at us. I saw Dolinski blink, but he did a good job of keeping his cool.

"Police officers, Mr. Lopez. We'd like to speak with you." I held my badge in front of his face.

Lopez looked at us menacingly with the large crescent wrench in his hand pointed at me. I used my left index finger to push it to the side. He relaxed.

I hadn't seen him in years, and his looks hadn't improved. His skin was a mottled tan and white stretched over his skull like puckered Saran Wrap. Both ears were disfigured, as if they had started to melt, and his hair—what was left of it—was scattered around his mostly bald head like the clumps of crabgrass in the lawn.

He gave me a good look for a long moment before saying, "Yeah, man, I remember jou. Saryent Yenkins, right? Jou drove a blue and white car around here."

I gave him a friendly smile. "It's lieutenant now, and yeah, you're right, it's been a long time since I was the sergeant in Bellport."

Lopez grabbed a straw pork-pie hat from the roof of his gold Chevy.

The wide cloth band was red with white flowers and green leaves. It clashed with his yellow Hawaiian shirt.

He dropped the little fedora on his head and took a six-inch cigar from his top pocket. He stripped off the clear wrapper and dropped it on the ground. A couple of fingers were missing on each hand, and the others were gnarled and deformed.

Lopez made a production out of lighting the cigar, and then tilting his head skyward, he blew out a cloud of smoke.

"So," he began, "what can I do for jou gennelmens? I ain't done nothing wrong…lately." He smiled—it looked repulsive.

"Nothing's wrong with you, Hector. We just wanted to ask you about Elizabeth. She works with us, and it seems like something's wrong with her. I've asked, but she says she's okay. I just can't believe that."

"Why are jou axing me? That one, she's a pain in my ass, man. Besides she's twenty-two now, no twenty-three. Yeah, twenty-three. She ain't my responsibility no more."

"We thought you may know something that would help us to help her," Joe said.

"No, man, I don't know nothin'." He did the head tilt thing again and sent another smoke signal into the atmosphere.

"How about your wife?" I asked. "Would Lizzie talk to her?"

"Who knows, man? She ain't here no more. She left me a couple years ago." He didn't seem overly concerned.

"Sorry to hear that," I said.

"No sweat, man. She was a pain in my ass, too. But who needs them, you know? I got me a big house and a good car. The neighborhood, it would be better if there wasn't so many low-class niggers, you know. But I like it here."

A mangy, brindle-colored mongrel loped from behind a neighbor's house and crossed the street, paying us no mind. I looked around at the scenery again.

"Yeah, a virtual garden spot. A real fuckin' paradise," I said. "But I can see how a gentleman like you might get upset if the neighbors didn't keep up appearances."

Lopez took that as a compliment.

Joe suppressed a smile, and then asked, "You know where we can find Lizzie's mother?"

"Not me, man." Puff, puff.

"How are your sons doing, Hector? I asked. "I haven't seen them since they were just kids."

"My sons? Shit, man, Jorge, the young one, he joined the fuckin' Navy. Stupid kid, he can't swim, and he joins the fuckin' Navy. And the big one, Indio, that pendejo, he got three more years to do in Ossining. Armed robbery—pendejo!" To emphasize certain words, he poked his cigar in the air at no one in particular.

We could have asked more, but we'd gotten nowhere, and I was tired of watching Hector punctuate his sentences with that burning phallic symbol. I thanked him for his time, and we left.

I put the Fury into gear and pulled away from the curb a little faster than necessary, scattering loose sand and gravel behind the wheels.

"And just why did you need me along for that?" Joe asked.

"Does Hopalong Cassidy go out and do his thing without Gabby Hayes?"

"Gabby Hayes?"

"I wanted to know what you thought of Hector."

"I'm glad we didn't meet him after lunch. Aside from the obvious, I don't know. How different is he from other guys like him? A shithead's a shithead, right?"

I nodded. "Speaking of lunch, how about the Carmen's River Inn? I need a martini."

"Sounds good. I see a vodka gimlet in my future."

* * * *

"Fifth Squad, Sergeant DeMarco."

I heard a familiar voice.

"Louie, Sam Jenkins. How's it goin'?"

"Hi ya, Sam. Long time no see."

"Yeah. You doin' all right, young feller?" I tossed in a compliment to the old man.

"Sure, couldn't be better, kid. I put my papers in last week. I'm going to retire next month. Thirty-six is enough for me."

"More than enough for anyone. Good luck to you. Hey, I'm looking

45

for Linda Ferrante. She around?"

"Yeah, she's in the office. Hang on, I'll switch the call."

Detective Linda Ferrante was one of the most compassionate cops I'd ever known, and one of the nicest people. I'd met her years ago when she worked in the Sex Crimes Unit. Linda was a damn good detective.

"Linda, how'd you like to do your old buddy a favor?"

"What do you have in mind, big boy?" She tried to sound like Mae West.

"Jeez, woman, don't put temptation in my path. I only need some professional help."

"I'm disappointed, but still listening."

I gave Linda the background on Liz Lopez.

I ended with, "I think she may have a problem talking freely to Artie Mandel—or any man. I think—just a guess now—she was sexually abused by her father. I'd like you to interview her. If anyone can get a story out of this girl, you can."

"Gee, thanks for your confidence. I hope I don't disappoint you. Have you talked to Frank O'Brien about this yet—or his boss?"

"They're next. If you've got the time, I'll square it away with them."

"If you've got the money, honey, I've got the time." Linda was a shameless flirt.

"Wow, I guess I'd better call you back."

* * * *

Investigator Frank O'Brien had two things going for him. He was a good cop, and his uncle was the former Chief Inspector. Frankie led a charmed life.

Ten years earlier, we worked together briefly. I called Frank where he now worked, the Applicant Investigation Unit. I suggested we get together and discuss his candidate.

"How's tomorrow?" he asked. "I've got a bunch of things to do in the Fifth Precinct. I could meet you for lunch."

"How about that sit-down deli on South Country, just west of Horseblock? You know it?"

"Sure, that works for me. What time?"

"A couple of my guys are going out to take pictures at a mafia funeral, but I'm basically free tomorrow, unless one of the big bosses calls down with something. Ring the office from the call box at Horseblock Road. I'll leave headquarters and be there ten minutes later."

* * * *

After a few minutes of catching up and a little gossip, Frankie and I got down to business.

"I haven't interviewed her old man yet," he said. "A real asshole, huh? I can't wait."

"Yeah, he's no Dale Carnegie graduate. Don't be surprised."

"You think her guns and tin would be safe in his house?" he asked.

"Probably not. I hope she moves if they promote her to PO."

"It's not a requirement."

"I know."

"Why do you think he abused her?" he asked

"I've got no evidence. I'm just reading the signs. You see how she acts. Something's definitely not kosher. That's why I'd like Linda to talk with her. She'll get the truth."

"Ferrante is that good?"

"Better."

"My boss says Liz should get another poly. He wants to give her the benefit of any doubt. He doesn't want anyone thinking we didn't give her every chance."

Frank didn't sound like he disagreed with his boss.

"Sam, I can't recommend denying her promotion without enough evidence to take to a section fifty hearing," he explained. "We can use the polygraph as a tool, not as proof of anything. And, I'll tell you, buddy, nobody on the second floor will want to use a by-pass on her. All the bosses want to promote CSAs. I think it's something to do with that consent decree the Feds hung around our necks."

All the chiefs and bigwigs had their offices on the second floor of the headquarters building. Our think-tank and brain-trust.

"Yeah, I understand," I said. "How about I coordinate with Linda and Artie? We'll let Linda do the pre-test interview her way. Then if she gets a story like I think she will, we'll have Artie run a few quick questions to explain away the report of deception from the first test. I think you and I should be on hand, too."

"Okay, sounds good. Give me a call, I'll be there."

* * * *

I made the arrangements. Linda would do the interview, Dr. Mandel the polygraph exam. Frankie and I would sit around in general support. I felt confident it would all work. And I had a card up my sleeve to play at the right moment.

Starting at ten that morning, Frank and I waited in the Chief of Detective's office while the action took place in the rooms used by the Polygraph Unit. Frank drank coffee and read over his cases. I shot the breeze with Gus Mazurki who had been a detective since before Noah started building boats.

At 11:15 Linda Ferrante walked in on us and seemed frazzled.

"Sam, my love, you owe me for this one." She shook her head, her dark brown hair looking a bit tousled. "We've got one messed up little girl there. Let's go somewhere private to talk." She tossed the jacket of her blue suit on the desktop next to me.

"Okay, kid, Frankie need to hear this, too?"

"Yeah. Let's use the commissioner's conference room. Can you square that?"

"Sure, give me a minute and a phone."

Ten minutes later we sat in padded swivel chairs, around an oval table, in a paneled room.

"Okay, Ferrante," I said, "you know I love you, but I can't wait any longer. What did you find out?"

She made a face. "Too much. You were right—good call. Her skank father started doing her when she was about eight. And he wasn't the only one. Apparently the whole Lopez clan is full of perverts. The old man passed her around to the two uncles. Bunch o' skells!"

Linda never fails to connect with her victims. Her slip was above her hemline, but her empathy showed.

I saw Frank close his eyes and shake his head.

I let out a quiet, "Jesus Christ."

Linda continued. "I'm surprised she's still this functional. At home she had no allies. She thinks the mother knew, and the best she could do for Liz was split. The brothers are a pair of shitheads who didn't lift a finger to help. She's never told anyone about this before. Talk about being all alone."

After watching Linda, I knew Hector Lopez should never go into a room alone with her.

"I've got to say, guys, if you don't feel sorry for Liz, hang it up."

Frankie nodded, looking like he had just been sapped.

"Is she still okay for Artie to do another test today?" I asked.

"She said she wants to get it over with, but Artie told her she should have time to calm down. She's scheduled to be back at one o'clock."

"Okay, then," I said. We've got an hour and a half. I'll buy you two lunch at the 10-18 Pub."

"Sammy, sweetheart, the lunch buffet at the 10-18 is free," Linda said.

"Okay, okay, I'll buy the drinks. I'm easy."

"Sam, if we weren't married to other people, I'd want to live with you. You're the most generous guy I've ever met."

"Mrs. Ferrante, your taste in men is exquisite, and I'd take you up on that if you weren't such a smartass."

She smiled. I wanted to break the tension.

Frank cleared his throat, a little too loudly. "Ah…guys, just pretend I'm not here."

* * * *

By ten-after-one Liz Lopez was connected to Artie Mandel's polygraph. Linda sat close, offering a modicum of moral support. I wanted to be present and sat against the wall—out of everyone's way. Frank O'Brien chose to stay outside.

"Okay, Liz," Mandel said. "This is going to be an easy one. Relax. Just four questions. No big deal here. From what Detective Ferrante told me, everything's out in the open now. I have no idea what you two spoke about, and that's okay. It's none of my business." Artie schmoozed it up to put her at ease. "I'll just verify for the record that everything's kosher, and you're home free. You doing okay?"

Liz nodded. Linda squeezed her hand. Liz didn't look particularly okay.

"Alright, here we go," Artie said.

The machine ticked away. Tiny pen-points on fragile arms scribed lines on the continuous roll of paper that slowly passed over the surface of the polygraph. Lizzie's heart rate, respiration, and galvanic responses were being recorded. As she responded to questions, the lines would either remain constant or go ballistic, depending on whether she spoke the truth or lied.

"Are you currently employed as a CSA?" Artie asked.

"Yes."

"Are you forty-five-years-old?"

"No."

No change in the more-or-less straight lines.

"During the time that you were interviewed by Detective Ferrante, did you tell even one lie?"

"No."

Still a good chart. Then he threw in an easy one for the peak of tension question.

"Do you want to be promoted to police officer?"

"Yes."

There was a slight waver, but Artie ignored it.

"Okay," he said, "I think we're finished."

I sat forward in my chair. "Wait," I said.

Artie, Linda and Liz looked at me, all waiting to see why I was throwing a monkey wrench at the operation.

"Leave the machine on for another minute," I said.

"What's going on, Loo?" Artie asked.

"Liz," I said, ignoring Mandel, "I have one more thing."

She looked at me like a deer caught in the headlights.

"Did you set your father on fire?"

The needles swung violently, like they might cut the paper in half. Lizzie's face contorted. Artie looked at me in disbelief. Linda looked like she could have cut my heart out.

"Artie," I said, "unplug your machine now, and give us a minute."

He switched off the polygraph and left the room. Linda took the clips off Lizzie's fingers and helped her remove the spiral cord from around her chest.

"Sam?" Linda said.

I held up a hand. It was my turn to speak.

"Liz, you've endured more than one person should ever have to deal with. Linda and I know that. We sympathize with you, but we have to know what happened. You have to get this out of your system so you can go on with your life."

She hung her head. Tears ran down her cheeks. Her classically beautiful face changed to a mask of pain and sorrow. I felt like I just shot her puppy.

She began to nod, but still said nothing.

"Liz, we're not looking to harm you." Linda picked up a ball I hadn't tossed. "What happened was long ago. You know enough about the law. Something like that has a statute of limitations. It happened more than five years ago, and no one can charge you. Your father can't try to punish you, and we don't want to. Do you understand?"

Liz nodded with a little purpose.

"Lizzie," I said. "What your father and uncles did is unforgivable. I can't change what happened. None of us can. I wish I could. But we can try to help you. Get this off your chest. It's like having a chain around you. Just say it. For years it's been eating away at you. You know it. We know it now, and no one else matters. Please, just tell us the truth."

Linda put her hand on my forearm to shut me up. Liz cried—a lot. She couldn't have spoken if she wanted to. We waited.

She began nodding again. As she nodded, she rhythmically rocked back and forth. She cried, sniffed, and finally took a tissue from the pocket of her slacks and dabbed her eyes. Someone might say they could feel her pain, but unless they were in her position, that's untrue.

Liz closed her eyes for a long moment. The turmoil inside her showed. She took a deep breath and began.

"He had been drinking all night," she said. "Rum, I think, I don't know. It was brown. He fell asleep smoking one of those big ugly cigars. Earlier that night he made me..."

She almost choked on her words. After a short pause, she began again. "My mother went to bed—she didn't care. She never cared. My brothers were out, I don't know where. I went to the living room. The TV was on—Johnny Carson, I think. It was late. I looked at my father, hating him for what he did to me. His cigar started to burn the arm of the chair. It smelled awful. I took his unfinished drink and poured it over his shirt. Then I took his lighter and made a fire with the TV Guide and threw it on him."

151 rum never left a nastier hangover.

The tears began again. She hid her face in her hands and sobbed. Linda put an arm around her shoulders and made motherly sounds. I sat there like a bump on a log. After a few moments, she continued.

"The flames started to spread, and he woke up. The chair was on fire. His clothes were on fire. He was screaming, waving his arms around. His hair caught on fire. He rolled over on the floor. I ran out, yelling for my mother."

She took a breath and sobbed softly.

"As soon as she got downstairs, she found him on the rug and took the blanket from the couch and began beating the flames. Finally she put him out and called 9-1-1. That's all I remember."

Linda held Liz. I put my hand on hers, and she pulled it away. After a few moments, I walked out and left the two women alone.

* * * *

"What the hell's going on in there?" Mandel asked.

"She's having a tough time. Linda's trying to calm her down. Do you have another test scheduled? Do we have to get her out?"

"No, I'm clear for the rest of the tour. Take your time."

I nodded. "Okay, good." I wasn't ready to listen to Dr. Mandel.

"By the way, that was an invalid question," he said, looking troubled that an interloper muscled in on his specialty.

"Yeah, I know the drill. I'm trying to get her to talk. I don't want to arrest her."

I turned and walked next door to the interview room looking for Frank O'Brien. I found him writing up another case. Diligence was one of his strong points.

"Listen, Frankie, we're having a real emotional time with her. I'll call you as soon as I can sort this out. You don't have to wait."

He nodded. "I'll be downstairs if you need me."

Mandel saw me and walked away, toward the coffee room next to the Robbery Unit. I stood there leaning against the wall, trusting Linda to do the right thing.

Ten minutes later, the door opened, and Linda asked me to join them. Liz looked like hell. Linda's face showed the stress of the moment and the sympathy she felt for the kid.

"Sam," Linda said, "Liz wants to know what happens next."

I looked at Liz trying not to seem confused, but I had nothing to tell her.

"Honestly, kid, it beats the hell outta me. I've never run across something like this before. And I didn't want to call O'Brien's boss, who might know what to do. I don't want him hear about this yet—if at all."

She just kept staring at me, no fear, no anger, no apprehension showed.

"Do you really want to be a cop?" I asked.

It took her a moment to respond. "I don't know."

"That would be a good thing to figure out."

She nodded.

"If you don't get promoted, would you stay a CSA or look for another job?"

"I don't know what else to do."

"CSA pay isn't very much."

She nodded.

"Is your car paid for?"

"No."

"You have any other financial obligations?"

"Some."

"If you stayed a CSA, would you have to continue living with your father?"

"I couldn't afford a place on my own."

"Has he…bothered you lately?"

"Not that way. After the fire… I don't think he can anymore."

That idea made me shiver.

"He used to hit me sometimes," she said, "especially if he got drunk."

"Does he still?" Linda joined the conversation.

"No. I told him I'd have someone…make him stop."

"You have a boyfriend?" Linda asked.

"No, he thought I meant a cop."

"Good," I said. "You won't ever have to put up with him again. Come to me if…" I let my offer trail off.

"Thanks," she said.

"I suppose you'd rather live on your own?"

"God, yes."

Her eye makeup had smeared, and black streaks ran down her cheeks. She looked beaten.

"Okay, I'll have to get back to you with a suggestion. I need time to find someone to help us. Do you have someplace to go if you took the rest of the day off?"

"My friend Belinda is off today. I could stay with her, but I don't have much sick time left."

"Don't worry. The time is on the house. I'll tell Nancy. Just don't discuss this with anyone, okay?"

"Okay, thanks."

"See you tomorrow?"

She nodded and left.

"Good job, Lin. Thank you," I said.

"I feel so sorry for her. What's going to happen?"

"Let's start by seeing if we can convince Dr. Mandel to keep his mouth shut."

* * * *

Dr. Noel Benson, a real doctor, not a polygraph examiner with a Hippocratic appearance, had been a police surgeon for more years than I'd been a cop. Once a respected chest cutter, arthritis had crippled his hands to the point where the only incision he felt comfortable making was on the Christmas turkey.

Several years earlier, he'd been appointed as chief of the county's Medical Health Department. One of his responsibilities was to coordinate medical and psychological examinations for police candidates.

Noel was a character. He looked like an aging star of a 1950's sitcom.

"Lieutenant, hello. It's been a long time, hasn't it? Good to see you." He spoke with a theatrical voice to match his appearance.

"Hello, Doctor. Good to see you, too."

We shook hands. He pointed me to a guest chair in front of his cluttered desk.

"Do you have a minute to hear a sad story?" I asked.

"You should be a writer, Lieutenant. Isn't that what they call a hook?"

"Maybe I should be a fisherman."

He chuckled.

"Tell me your story." He settled into his big chair.

I began, and when I came near the end, I said, "Now I'd like to get hypothetical."

He smiled; no one ever *really* gets hypothetical.

I told him the punch line about Liz setting Hector ablaze. Benson winced as if he could feel the heat.

"The poor man!" He looked shocked and eyed me carefully.

"I'm more inclined to say, 'Poor girl.'"

"That's what I wanted to hear you say, Lieutenant." He grinned and fingered his paisley bow tie.

"Maybe you should be the cop."

"You people deal with too much blood and gore."

"Yes, right." I let that one go, "I'm not concerned about the man. It's been almost twelve years since the fire. He is what he is. It's what happens to the girl that matters to me."

"She needs psychotherapy…badly."

"So do I, but here I sit."

That got a laugh.

"Still speaking hypothetically, Doctor, if you and the psychologist had this information, but she's able to pass her written MMPI, would she pass the psych exam?"

"I couldn't possibly know at this point."

I wanted a more hopeful answer.

"Let's say this information was the only detractor in her psychological work-up. Would it automatically disqualify her, even though she's a good employee, capable of being a police officer and deserving of a promotion?"

"Are you asking me to overlook something for your employee?"

"You're getting old, my friend, but your hearing is still good."

That one got me a genuine belly-laugh. *Maybe I should look for a part-time job as a comic in the Catskills*

"You're not asking a medical opinion, Lieutenant, you're presenting me with a moral dilemma."

"They're a dime a dozen in my business. I'm asking how far your discretion can stretch."

His eyes got a little wider, but he let me finish.

"As a cop, I try to anticipate how things might go in a courtroom. I always have the discretion to do one of several things. I'm looking at this and thinking perhaps the young lady was punished prior to her questionable act."

He raised his eyebrows almost two inches. "Questionable?" It sounded as if he disagreed with my use of words.

"If I caught a father forcibly raping his daughter, the law allows me to use deadly force to prevent or terminate that rape. In my language, Doctor, I'd light him up, but not with a Bic."

"I see your point." His tension softened.

"I also follow timely court dispositions. Recently, people have used long-term abuse as a defense and were acquitted of murder. The statute of limitations is long over on this assault. The father never made a complaint. I believe he was too drunk to know what really happened. He sexually abused her earlier that night. She was only eleven years old, for God's sake." I settled back in my chair, feeling satisfied at having presented a strong case.

"The fact remains…" He raised his eyebrows again, but only an inch. "Let me think about this…hypothetically, of course."

"One last thought. If she had been arrested as a juvenile, and even though determining a child's level of culpability is often difficult, let's say some zealous prosecutor charged her with attempted murder, and she received a maximum sentence. She would have been released five years ago—her debt completely paid."

He nodded. His expression showed him carefully considering what I said.

"I'll call you back."
"I can't ask for more."

* * * *

The next morning the doctor called.
"Lieutenant, is there an official document outlining this hypothetical confession we spoke of?"
"No, nothing is on paper."
"How many people are privy to what the girl said?"
"If I were that fiction writer who used the hook on you, I'd say only two characters heard anything."
"Other than that, we have only an open-ended polygraph report indicating unexplained deception?" he asked.
"That end was sewn shut when Miss Lopez told Detective Ferrante the incidents she failed to disclose during the first test were the incestuous assaults her father and uncles subjected her to."
"That's your official stance?"
"This isn't my stance to take. Her investigation is being handled by someone in another unit. But I believe I can confidently say, nothing about the hypothetical fire will ever be published."
"I make no promises, Lieutenant. She must take and pass the medical and psychological exams."
"I understand. She may have flat feet or high blood pressure. Those are not my concern."
"We have the young lady on our list of appointments. She'll get her letter shortly, but you may tell her she should be here at 8 a.m., July 1st. Then we'll let the chips fall where they may."
"I think you're a stand-up guy, Doctor."
"Why, Lieutenant, I don't know what you're talking about."

* * * *

Linda Ferrante and I sat in my car in front of the 5th Squad building. We watched the traffic on Waverly Avenue and drank coffee.
"Artie never actually heard anything about the fire," I said. "He's using your interview notes to write up his report for the second test. That first implied deception is accounted for and seems inconsequential now."
"Artie's good like that."

"I spoke to Frank O'Brien," I said. "He likes Liz, thinks she's one of the better CSAs. He's okay with never knowing more than her admission about hiding the sex abuse. Anyone who reads his case summary would understand her being embarrassed. He feels sorry for her. I'm glad those cases are confidential."

"You're getting compassionate in your old age."

"Yeah, I'm almost forty. It's time to be a softie."

"Not so old. I think you're still a tough-guy."

"You're the only one left, kiddo. You okay with what I'm doing?"

"Don't worry about me, boss. I agree with you. I think she'd be as good a cop as any kid her age."

I finished my coffee and dropped the cup into a paper bag. Linda still had hers to finish.

"Good. Now she can go for her tests and take her chances, without certain information becoming public."

"You're a good guy, Jenkins. Everybody says you take care of your people."

"You're a good accomplice. And you settled for just a cup of coffee. I would have bought you lunch."

"Another time."

"You're not only a good woman, but a cheap date. Who could ask for anything more?"

"Suppose my father owned a liquor store?"

"Wow, now you're talkin'."

THE END

Angel of the Lord

Wayne Zurl

Dedication

To Audie Daily who keeps our appliances in good repair, but hasn't committed any murders.

Angel of the Lord
Wayne Zurl

The rain never stopped. From early June through late August, it poured or drizzled almost every day. I thought if I stood still too long I might begin to mold. It reminded me of the monsoons in Southeast Asia.

Drops of rain falling from the brim of my cap were exceeded only by the young woman's tears.

"When did you see the boy last?" I asked.

"Right after breakfast. He went into the living room to watch TV, and I started doing laundry in the basement."

"And when you came upstairs he was gone?"

More tears rolled over her cheeks as she stood there, wringing her hands. "Yes."

"Was your door locked?"

"Lord have mercy, no."

"Is your son's rain jacket here?"

She shrugged and cried a little more.

"Let's look," I suggested.

We walked to the mud room off the kitchen. A small hooded jacket hung on one of the five pegs over an antique wooden chair not six feet from the back door. A small pair of bright blue rubber Wellingtons sat on the floor.

"You call for him outside?"

"Of course. I ran all around."

Without the puffy eyes and fear scarring her face, Emily Suttles would have been an attractive brunette.

"And then you called 9-1-1?"

"Yes."

"What was he watching?"

"I don't know. He knows how to work the TV."

"You turn it off?"

"One of the policemen did."

"Let's take a look."

She stared at me as if I had two heads. "Why?"

"Indulge me."

Back in the living room, Emily picked up the remote control and turned on a flat screen about the size of a stretch van. The American Movie Classics channel came on playing a scene from *Halloween 4.*

"Did you or the cops look through the house?" I asked.

"Yes, of course."

"All over?"

"Every room."

"Slowly or quick?"

"Quick. I was frantic."

"Let's try again. Where's Elijah's room?"

"Upstairs." Emily began to look impatient. "I know he's not there."

We walked upstairs anyway. I looked under the bed. Nothing. The boy's mother called his name. More nothing. I opened the closet. Huddled in the left corner, leaning against the wall, four-year-old Elijah Suttles slept peacefully, a small flashlight in his right hand. I shook his knee.

"Hey, partner, you doing okay in here?"

He opened his eyes, blinked rapidly, and looked frightened.

"Take it easy, son. I'm a policeman. Your mom couldn't find you and asked for some help."

"Jesus have mercy, Elijah," his mother said, "you 'bout scared me half ta death. You come out here right now, young man."

"Go slow, Mrs. Suttles. He probably had a good reason to hide in here. Didn't you, son?"

The little boy nodded, but still looked scared.

"Something happen on the TV?"

Another nod.

"Ready to come out now?"

The boy stuck out a hand, and I pulled. Once on his feet, he scrambled to his mother and locked onto her leg, mumbling an apology.

"Some of these slasher movies scare me, too," I said. "He just ran from the killer on the screen. Wasn't a bad idea."

Emily Suttles hugged her son, looked at me, and said, "Thank you."

"I'll call the three officers and let them know your son's safe."

I switched on the ignition in my unmarked Crown Victoria and keyed the microphone. "Prospect-one to headquarters and all units. The missing child has been found. Resume patrol. Five-twelve, close out the call at 1015 hours."

PO Johnny Rutledge acknowledged. "10-4, Prospect-one."

"Five-oh-nine, I copy that," Billy Puckett said.

After a long moment of silence, Sergeant Bettye Lambert, our desk officer, broke in. "Unit 513, five-one-three, do you copy?"

No answer.

"Anyone know 513's 10-35?" I asked.

"Joey was goin' house ta house, east end o' the street," Puckett said.

"I'm probably the closest," I said. "I'll check."

Just as I shifted into reverse, PO Joey Gillespie spoke on the radio.

"513 ta Prospect-one. Boss, ya gonna need ta see this. 1175 Benny Stillwell Road, obvious 10-5."

10-5 is our brevity code for a homicide.

* * * *

Two men lay face down on the kitchen floor. One with a shaved head made it easy to see the small caliber bullet hole at the base of his skull—a .25 perhaps or more likely a .22. Blood trickled from the wound down past his right ear, over a thick neck, and onto the Mexican tile floor. The other victim's blood oozed to his left. Funny, the little details you notice at the scene of a murder.

"You call crime scene and the ME?" I asked.

"Yessir, had Miss Bettye do it right after I called ya."

I nodded and looked around the kitchen of a relatively new and expensive home. "Big house."

Joey Gillespie nodded.

"At least 4,000 square feet," I guessed. "And quality. These guys had bucks."

He nodded again and looked a little queasy.

"The air hasn't come on recently. In this humidity blood tends to stink quicker. Smell bother you?"

"Yessir, I ain't used ta this."

"Nobody gets used to it, kid. You just learn to ignore it."

"I guess."

"You search the rest of the house?"

"Jest looked on the first floor ta see if there was anybody here."

"Basement?"

"Nosir. On a slab."

"Let's go upstairs."

I drew my old Smith & Wesson from the holster on my right hip, and Joey pulled out his .40 caliber Glock.

"Look around, and pay attention. Don't watch me. There's probably no one here, but we'll do this by the numbers."

"Yessir. I'm right behind ya."

We made a quick sweep of the first floor, opening all the closets before ascending the stairs. The landing above left us in a hallway with what looked like four bedrooms, two baths and two closet doors. We found nothing in the guest johns or closets. A lack of personal property in three of the bedrooms led me to believe they were set also aside for guests. We looked further in the master suite and discovered two closets holding clothing for two different people.

"I guess the two guys slept t'gether," Joey said.

"Yep."

"Strange, huh?"

"Not strange, just a minority."

"Uh-huh."

Two car doors slammed out front.

"Let's see who's here," I suggested.

Jackie Shuman and David Sparks, crime scene investigators from the Blount County Sheriff's Office, had arrived and stood in the foyer holding cameras and forensic kits. Moments later, Deputy Medical Examiner Morris Rappaport and his assistant Earl Ogle pulled up in the morgue wagon.

"How'd ya find these two?" Jackie asked of no one in particular.

"I's checkin' the neighborhood for a missin' child," Joey said. "Got no answer here, but there was two cars in the driveway and the garage was closed. Figgered someone's home, so I walked 'round back and seen them layin' here on the floor."

"Nice wheels out there," David said.

"Audi S7 and an F-Type Jag," I said. "Pushing a hundred grand apiece."

"And they're relatively new, right?" Morris asked.

"The Jag's new, and the Audi's not far behind."

"With these two sporty drivers, why do you suppose there's an oil spot on the concrete driveway?"

"Good question, Mo," I said. "Something for our ace evidence technicians to explore."

"We'll git'er done," Jackie said.

"And take pictures of this table top. Someone ruined a nice antique."

Jackie looked closer at the numbers someone crudely scratched into the mellow wood finish.

"Thirteen thirteen," he said. "Wonder what that means?"

"Two unlucky numbers," Morris said.

"Two unlucky guys," I said. "Has to mean something. Finding out will keep me from playing in the traffic."

* * * *

We worked on the case for six days and knew very little other than Chad Higgins and Lance Quayle were thirty-nine and forty-one years old, respectively. Both men had good jobs, working in the financial sector of Knoxville, and were openly gay. Those who could provide information said they had been a monogamous couple for almost five years. Nothing led us to believe either one had any drug, alcohol, or gambling problems. No one seemed to hate them.

"Anything else I can check for you?" Bettye Lambert asked.

"I hate to admit I'm baffled, but we've done it all. The autopsy only confirmed the obvious, and forensics gave us diddly squat."

"Is this what they call a random act of violence?"

"Might be a hate crime we'll never solve. Might be a love triangle no one knew about. Maybe they saw Big Vito whack somebody, and he was afraid they'd talk."

"We have someone named Big Vito in Prospect?"

65

"You're too smart for your own good."

"Thank ya, darlin'."

Bettye showed me a smile designed to cloud men's minds.

"I wish I knew what thirteen thirteen means. The killer didn't scratch it on the table for no reason."

"No crime on file with a similar act. I'll keep working on that."

The phone rang, and Bettye answered. She listened, scribbled down some information, asked a few questions and ended by saying, "We'll have a car come right over."

"Something good?" I asked.

"A Mrs. Pitts says she hasn't seen her neighbor in several days. His car's in the garage, and there haven't been any lights on at night."

"She ever hear about vacations and air travel?"

"You can be so snotty at times. I'll send Junior to check it out."

"Super idea."

Ten minutes later, the radio crackled.

"501, headquarters, request permission to break a window and enter this house."

"For what reason, five-zero-one?" Bettye asked.

"Tag on the car here comes back ta Asher Henderson. That's the guy Knox County convicted fer swindlin' all those people in his investment scheme. He ain't been sentenced yet, and the neighbor says he always leaves a timer on the lights if he ain't home at night."

I stood next to Bettye, listening to Junior Huskey's transmission. Bettye looked at me for an answer. I leaned over and keyed the mic.

"Stand-by, 501, I'll be right there."

"10-4," Junior said.

"What do you think?" Bettye asked.

"I don't. That's why I break into people's homes."

"You just don't want Junior to get into trouble."

"When I retire and they make you chief, I hope you don't act like me."

"Few people could or would act like you, Sammy."

* * * *

Asher Henderson's brick home wasn't particularly large, but

situated on a spacious lot in a ritzy neighborhood. It had great curb appeal and looked expensive. Junior's white and blue patrol car sat in the driveway. I parked on the blacktop road.

As we walked around back to the kitchen door, I said, "I'm surprised Mrs. Pitts is still talking with this con man"

"Told me he's always been a good neighbor," Junior said. "I guess she didn't invest with him."

A dead bolt made it impossible for me to jimmy the door open, but one of the six panes of glass allowed me to make a relatively small mess by smashing it with my cast aluminum flashlight.

I flipped the lock and used Junior's memo book to brush aside the shards of glass so we could enter the house, turning on lights as we progressed through the rooms.

In an upstairs room set aside as an office, we found one of the most bizarre murders I'd ever seen.

Henderson sat in an overstuffed leather swivel chair behind a large oak desk. A single small caliber hole scarred his forehead. A narrow trail of blood had drizzled down between his eyes, over his nose and cheek, and disappeared under his chin. The left side of his brown and white Tattersall shirt was stained red, while a fistful of dollar bills filled his mouth.

"Shoot!" Junior said.

"Looks like someone did."

The large calendar and other common paraphernalia had been swept off the desktop and onto the floor. The numbers twenty-two and two had been scratched into the wood surface."

"What's that mean?" Junior asked.

"Means we've got a serial killer in beautiful downtown Prospect."

Before the regular crew of forensics and pathology investigators arrived, I asked Junior to move his car. As I suspected, a fresh oil spot marked the concrete apron in front of the garage. I doubted that Asher Henderson's new S-500 Mercedes had sprung a leak.

* * * *

I called Furlan Atchley, a weasel of a man at the Knox County District Attorney's office, bureau chief for major cases.

"I suppose you heard that your Ponzi scammer, Asher Henderson, bought the farm in Prospect yesterday."

"I have. What do you know so far?"

"Very little, except a factor not included in the press release tends to indicate this is related to his swindling."

"Oh?"

"Besides a bullet in the brain, he had a mouthful of greenbacks."

"Says a lot, but doesn't make yer job any easier."

"How so?"

"I've got a hundred and twenty-six complainants named in his indictment. His money is somewhere off-shore and he's not saying where. Even with his death, it's doubtful anyone will ever get back anythin' close to their full investment."

"Beautiful. And I've got two more victims probably killed by the same gun. Tests should be back today, but five will get you ten I've got three bodies and one killer. The names Chad Higgins or Lance Quayle mean anything to you? They worked at a brokerage house on Walnut Street in the old city."

"No bells, but I'll check. Y'all see any connection with Henderson?"

"Not yet. The numbers twenty-two two mean anything in Henderson's case?"

"Twenty-two two, not two-two-two?"

"Either way."

"Twenty-two two sounds like a chapter and verse from the Bible."

"Don't you need to know what book the chapter came from?"

"Sure."

"So what book has a famous chapter twenty-two?"

"How should I know? I go to church, but I'm no biblical scholar."

"How about thirteen-thirteen?"

"Same. Where'd that turn up?"

"At the Higgins-Quayle murders."

"If these three aren't connected, you've got a serial killer down there in the foothills."

"Gee whiz, I wish I had thought of that."

He let my bit of sarcasm slide and seemed to have taken no offense. I've always thought it's impossible to offend a lawyer.

"Any indication Henderson was gay?" I asked.

"Not even close. He liked to spend money and have a good time. Hot and cold runnin' women. I assume your other victims were homosexuals?"

"Lived together."

"Doesn't sound like I can help you, but I'll have the lead detective on our case give you a call."

"Good. Thanks."

"Okay. Keep me informed."

"Sure thing."

I wondered why Atchley hadn't called me first. It's not every day your star defendant gets killed just before sentencing.

* * * *

Television, movies, and literature would like you to believe that all crimes are solved after finding an elusive clue or through a display of sheer brilliance by the fictional detective. In truth, cops solve crimes by plodding along the streets looking for information. But not all sources of information are creepy little characters or junkies who most people avoid like the plague.

After getting a decent idea from Furlan Atchley, I drove to Saint Michael's Roman Catholic Church to see Father Declan McGill, who once helped me with an important and interesting case.

"Oh, saints persarve us," he said, trying to imitate one of his Irish ancestors. "We've got a Protestant in our midst."

Declan took a few steps down the aisle of the church and stuck out a hand for me to shake.

"More of a pagan, actually," I said.

He smiled, and I wondered how many female congregants wouldn't like to engage in an afternoon of sin with the handsome young priest.

"Your Barry Fitzgerald accent is getting better all the time," I said.

"I was hoping you'd say so. I practice a lot. Let's sit down."

We slid into one of the pews and got as comfortable as possible.

"I see you in the papers occasionally and quite often on WNXX. Makes me think you might have a friend in the television business," he said.

"It's good to have friends. Take you, for instance. You're my pipeline to Heaven."

He tossed his head back and laughed. "I'm honored. Did you come to shoot the breeze, or can I help with something?"

"A lesson in Biblical verse, perhaps."

I told him about the two incidents and how the killer left what may have been references to the bible.

"Your first two men were openly homosexual and the killer scratched thirteen thirteen into a tabletop near the bodies. Sounds like he wanted to leave a clue and an easy one. Genesis 13:13 refers to the sins of those at Sodom and Gomorrah. The killer might see gay men as Sodomites. If properly written, it should have been thirteen colon thirteen."

"I guess he was in too much of a hurry to add the proper punctuation and make it easy for me."

"The convicted felon and 22:2 probably refers to Exodus. I may be misquoting, but it says something like this, 'If a thief is found and is smitten that he die, no blood shall be shed for him.'"

"A bullet between the eyes certainly constitutes being smitten."

* * * *

And so it came to pass that six days later, when I thought God was supposed to be busy creating man and woman, the killer struck again, eliminating one of those females.

The anonymous phone call to county 9-1-1 at 7:30 in the morning had been timed just right. We don't open the office at Prospect PD until 8 a.m. Between 7:30 and 8 o'clock, most of the patrol cops of the world are winding down after a midnight tour, doing last minute paperwork, gassing their cars or completing the little things necessary before going off-duty and turning their sectors over to the day crew. They're usually close to their headquarters or relief points and not patrolling. So, anyone wanting to get away from a crime scene with minimum chance of being seen by a police officer would be well advised to do it during those times when the shifts are changing. This information is not secret, and the bad guys all know it.

When I arrived at the old house on Doc Beasley Road at 8:30, I found enough vehicles present to start a used car lot. In addition to a matched pair of Prospect PD cruisers parked on the roadway, a red GMC pickup and brown Ford Explorer sat on the gravel driveway with a Rural Metro ambulance behind them.

Inside the house, PO Jamey Hawkins stood with his thumbs hooked over his gun belt, looking tired after working the midnight tour. Bobby John Crockett stood next to him, holding a clipboard with the crime scene log attached. On the couch, a dark-haired man in his late-forties sat next to a woman in her mid-fifties. Unless Mother Nature was trying to play tricks on me, they looked enough alike to be brother and sister.

Hawkins motioned for me to join him in the kitchen.

"Guy on the couch is Charlie Cousins," he said. "Woman is his sister Joyce Hamblen. I got his name from the mother who was locked in the basement."

A woman laid face down on the linoleum kitchen floor, her mousy brown hair matted with blood. A puddle of dried blood started under her ear and spread for more than a foot to her right. A broken leaded glass shade had been tossed against the wall near the back door and a bronze lamp base, a little more than twelve inches tall, lay on the floor, also discolored with the victim's blood.

A minor commotion from the opposite side of the room drew our attention to the basement stairs as two paramedics wrangled a gurney up the steps. When they hit the kitchen floor, I saw a white haired woman strapped onto the litter, an oxygen mask covering most of her wrinkled face.

"She gonna make it?" I asked the female attendant.

She shrugged. "Maybe."

"Was she attacked?"

"No signs of a beating. She's diabetic and really out of it. Hasn't had any attention for a day or more."

"Tell the ER crew she's part of my crime scene."

She nodded. "Sure. If you look at where she had to live, you'll see another crime. I wouldn't keep pigs in a place like that."

"Thanks."

She nodded again and helped her partner wheel the patient out of the room.

"The old lady tell you anything?" I asked Hawkins.

"She was only semi-conscious. Just said call her son Charlie Cousins." Jamey shook his head. "She's only got one leg, and the other one doesn't look in good shape. I didn't spend much time downstairs. The stink could gag a maggot. Ya need a Scott Pack to breath down there."

"Who's the victim?"

"Jane Cousins, sister of those two inside." He pointed toward the living room with his chin.

"I guess calling Jane the mother's caregiver would be a gratuitous statement?"

"A zookeeper treats the animals better."

I glanced around the kitchen and wasn't surprised to find the numbers twenty twenty scratched on a cabinet door.

"You know much about the scriptures?" I asked.

"Not hardly."

"Looks like our Bible thumping killer struck again"

I used an oxygen resuscitator switched to inhalant when I descended the basement steps. To confirm the statements made by the medic and Jamey Hawkins, I removed the mask and took a breath. Neither had exaggerated.

A metal framed twin-sized bed sat with the head against a wall. A tubular aluminum and plastic portable toilet was only a couple feet away near an old scarred up chest-of-drawers. I didn't think the chamber pot had been emptied lately. The rest of the basement looked like a seldom used shop with a slop sink near a homemade workbench, a washing machine and dryer, and a chest freezer.

A wood roach as big as an MG Midget scurried from under the bed and disappeared behind the freezer. The dead bodies of his former colleagues were scattered everywhere along with mouse droppings and dust bunnies. Rank dampness heightened the smell of urine and sickness.

If Jane Cousins' brother and sister cared anything for their mother and they connected with my other three victims, I'd place them at the top of my suspect list.

The living room looked cleaner than the basement, but not by much. I opted not to sit on one of the upholstered chairs and stood next to

Bobby Crockett. Jamey Hawkins had gone off-duty.

"How did your sister get custody of your mother?" I asked.

Charlie shook his head, looking disgusted. Joyce answered.

"She talked Momma into giving her power of attorney. Jane sold Momma's house and said she'd use the money to care for her."

"Did you know about the conditions downstairs?"

Charlie nodded and Joyce answered again. "We did, and we complained to Social Services. Those fools called first for an appointment to inspect the place, and Jane had time to clean things up. That was a long time ago."

"They thought it was okay to keep your mother locked away in the basement?"

"They said there were bathroom facilities and considered it adequate.'

"A portable john and slop sink was a bathroom?" I sounded surprised even to myself.

Bobby said, "Lord have mercy."

"I came here once," Charlie said, "and tried to take Momma with me. Only she wouldn't come, and Jane chased me out with a frying pan sayin' if I trespassed again she'd call y'all and git me arrested."

Joyce added, "If this is how she planned to care for Momma, that house money would last hundreds o' years."

"You plan on putting Mom in a nursing home?" I asked.

"Now that Jane's gone, I guess we can," Charlie said.

"The house money still in your mother's name?"

"No, sir. She gave it to Jane for tax purposes."

I'm no accountant, but that didn't sound exactly right to me.

"Are you two Jane's next of kin?"

"She's divorced years now. Never had no kids. Took back her maiden name. We don't know if she's got a will."

"Know anyone named Chad Higgins or Lance Quayle?"

Charlie shook his head. Joyce said, "No. Should we?"

"How about Asher Henderson?"

Charlie, the man of few words, shook his head again. Joyce said, "Sounds familiar, but I don't know from where."

"He's been in the news lately."

73

She nodded. "The one who cheated all those people out of their savin's?"

"That's the one."

Charlie perked up.

"I've seen him on the TV news," Joyce said.

"Either of you invest with him?"

"Invest?" Joyce said. "Honey, we look like Donald Trump and Marla Maples?"

"Your mother?"

They shook their heads.

"I guess neither of you do business with a brokerage house in Knoxville?"

"Got a bank account with First Tennessee," Charlie said.

"I invest in my five grandchildren," Joyce said.

"Okay," I said. "Officer Crockett is going to speak with you some more and take statements. Don't be offended when he asks where you've been for the last twenty-four hours."

They nodded, and I walked outside. The morgue wagon had just pulled up, and the big white crime scene SUV was coming down the road.

* * * *

While the evidence technicians and ME's team processed the murder scene, I dialed my direct line to God and explained the new developments.

"Twenty twenty doesn't sound familiar, so let me turn on my computer and see what I can find," Father Declan said.

"You have a computerized Bible?"

He laughed. "Welcome to 21st century religion."

I faked a Tennessee accent. "Lord have mercy. Ain't nuthin' sacred?"

"You're starting to sound like a local." He laughed again. "From what you described, I'm willing to bet we're dealing with the 5th Commandment here."

Computer keys ticked away in the background.

"Refresh my memory," I said.

He sighed. "Most *children* know that's 'Thou shalt honor thy father and mother.' Your victim fell down on the job."

"That's an understatement."

He paused for a long moment. "Here we go, Proverbs 20:20. A perfect fit. 'If one curses his father or mother, his lamp will be put out in utter darkness.'"

"A lamp put Jane Cousins out permanently."

Declan paused once more. I assumed he was reading again.

"Ooo, look at this one. Good thing birds weren't involved."

"Birds?"

"30:17 says, 'The eye that mocks a father and scorns to obey a mother will be picked out by the ravens of the valley and eaten by vultures.'"

"Yuck. I'm glad our killer doesn't have a pet vulture."

* * * *

I left Bobby John and the rest of the team to handle the crime scene, and I headed toward Blount Memorial Hospital, hoping to speak with Pauline Cousins. An admissions clerk for the ER gave me a doctor's name and pointed me in the right direction where I found a young man with a blond crew cut wearing sage green scrubs and shocking silver sneakers.

"Mrs. Cousins in shape to answer a few questions?"

He finished chewing on a Snickers bar and shook his head.

"You're too late. She died fifteen minutes ago."

"Lack of insulin?"

"That and many other factors. General poor health, poor nutrition, lack of reasonable hygiene care and her leg was so ulcerated we were thinking amputation. But no one figured she'd survive an operation." He shrugged. "She passed quickly."

"I'll save the family a few bucks and order an autopsy."

"Thought you might, so I sent her downstairs. You going to prosecute someone for her condition?"

"The daughter was responsible for that, and she was murdered. The killer locked the basement door on the old woman. I doubt she could have gotten to a phone, but I might be able to squeak in a felony murder charge for Pauline's death during the commission of the other pre-meditated murder. Pauline is at least a reckless manslaughter."

"Hell of a thing." He popped the last piece of Snickers into his mouth. "See ya."

* * * *

I called Jackie Shuman and asked him to let Crockett break the news of Pauline's death to Charlie and Joyce after they finished writing their statements.

"You got it, boss man," Jackie said.

"You get a chance to check the driveway for another infamous oil spot?"

"I had them move their ve-hickles, but there's so much little trash in the gravel I couldn't see anything like the drips we found on the ce-ment driveways."

"You get anywhere with those two samples?"

"Sure. Kinda old 10W-40 oil."

"I'll bet that narrows it down to less than a hundred thousand vehicles."

"Sorry."

"Do me another favor?"

"Sure."

"Get your boss to find out where the phone call to county 9-1-1 came from."

"You got it."

* * * *

I returned to Prospect PD and dropped down into the chair next to Bettye's desk like I had just finished a seventeen mile road march with a forty pound rucksack on my back.

"You looked frazzled." She smiled, and her hazel eyes sparkled.

"I need a vacation."

"And just who will find this serial killer if you fly off to Hawaii or some such place?"

"Alaska."

"What?"

"I'd rather go to Alaska. I'm not fond of heat."

She wrinkled up her nose. "Whatever. Before you get too comfortable, go upstairs and see the mayor. He called down a few minutes after I told Trudy about the new murder. He sounds…upset."

I trudged up the marble staircase of the municipal building, walked a few steps to the right and pushed open one of the glass doors that opened to the anteroom of the mayor's office. His secretary, Trudy Connor, smiled and buzzed his intercom. I turned the knob on one of the oversized raised panel oak doors just before Ms. Connor gave me the okay to enter. Her smile changed to a frown at my lack of formality.

Ronnie Shields is fifteen years younger than me, has a little boy face that will keep him young-looking until he's ninety and sports a slightly long, styled hairdo that looks like it's been fiberglassed into place.

He sat behind a mahogany desk large enough to play a game of Pee Wee football on it, tapping the eraser end of a pencil against his left index finger.

"Morning," I said.

He nodded, but not a hair moved. "Mornin', Sam."

It was his dime. I sat in one of the green leather guest chairs and waited.

"Bettye told me y'all have another murder. That makes four victims, right?"

"Actually, five."

His eyes widened, and he stopped tapping.

"The killer locked his target's mother in the basement. She died as a probable result."

"Lord have mercy, Sam. When y'all gonna ketch this killer?"

"So far nothing connects the victims, and he…or she's left little in the way of trace evidence. I wish I could be more optimistic, but…" I let my thought trail off.

Ronnie sighed. "The council held a meetin' last night to discuss this."

I frowned, knowing nothing good comes from the council when they start thinking.

"They wondered when you were gonna request he'p from the county or the TBI."

Ronnie generally means well, so I didn't jump on him immediately.

"The county's got a couple of good detectives I wouldn't mind using to help out, but they've got their own cases to handle, and without any promising undeveloped leads, they'd have little to work on. If you want the Tennessee Bureau of Investigation to come blustering in here smirking like they've got a suspect in their back pocket, go ahead and call them. Besides adding a bunch of investigators—whose talents have yet to be proven to me—they would have no more ideas than we do. Look, Ronnie, everything points to a religious maniac randomly picking targets. I'm sure he fancies himself God's vigilante out to rid the world of sinners and would love to be recognized as such. They all want recognition. They're nuts. Sooner or later he'll slip up. It's inevitable."

"But what if he kills again?"

"Serial killers are nothing new. Big departments like New York, Atlanta, Chicago, L.A., have all had them. Task forces bigger than the entire Blount County Sheriff's Office have worked on their cases, and people kept getting killed. Manpower doesn't guarantee a quick arrest."

Ronnie dropped his eyes. "Sam, the council would like some results."

The straw that broke the camel's back. "Screw the council. It's like telling the director of health services they want a cure for cancer."

He took a quick look at me, I guess, to see if I'd turned red.

"The next time you talk to those people, Ronnie, tell them I wouldn't dream of suggesting how to run their full-time businesses. They should keep their noses out of mine."

My voice had gotten so loud I expected Ms. Connor might burst through the door hoping to protect her mayor.

"Now, Sam, don't go getting' excited, please. They jest figgered . . ."

I interrupted him. "And why, if they are so concerned, didn't they invite me to this meeting to explain what we're doing?"

"Well, uh, I guess they jest wanted ta talk in private."

"Sure. I'll repeat my last suggestion. Screw the council." I sat back in the green chair and folded my arms across my chest. Sam Jenkins, outraged police chief.

"How 'bout your friends at the FBI? That I-talian feller, what's his name? Could ya git he'p from them?"

"His name's Ralph Oliveri. Most murders aren't federal crimes. If I could prove the Higgins-Quayle murders were hate crimes, they might be interested."

"Ya mean 'cause they were *homa-sexurals*?"

"Correct."

Ronnie's eyes showed a spark of hope. "Would ya consider that?"

I wasn't quite ready to roll over.

"I'll consider it. By the way, speaking of feds. Bettye has already used the federal database showing documented MOs. It's called VICAP. She's found nothing related to our circumstances."

"Too bad, but good. I mean, real fine. Yessir, real fine. Y'alls are using federal resources, jest like the FBI might."

I had nothing more to say. So, I waited. A long moment passed. Ronnie looked uncomfortable with the silence.

"Thanks for stoppin' in, Sam. Y'all will keep me informed, right?"

I stood and nodded. "Sure thing, boss."

On the way out I said, "Ms. Connor, I think the mayor needs a drink."

Not five minutes after I got back to the office, my cell phone blasted out a musical ringtone. I usually feel a pleasant spark of nostalgia when I hear the Stones do *Paint it Black*, but I really wasn't in the mood.

When I saw the familiar number on caller ID, I softened up a little.

"Are you avoiding me, Mr. Jenkins?" she asked.

"Rachel, sweetheart, you're my favorite reporter. You know that's not true."

"Not just a TV reporter, buddy, senior news anchor."

"Picky, picky, picky. Haven't I sent you all the poop from group before the press releases went out?"

Her voice changed. "Yes, but you haven't called with any updates."

I felt a little embarrassed. "Uh, mainly because . . ."

"You don't know anything new?" She sounded amazed.

"Sad but true."

"Wow, I'm surprised."

"Oh, well."

"I'm afraid *I* have some bad news for *you*," she said. "And because of it, I'll ask you a favor."

"Uh-oh."

"Allan Peters aired a special report this morning. It seems he found out about those Bible references and named the killer 'Angel of the Lord.'"

I let out a long breath and shook my head. "Why not the Hillside Strangler? Jeez, I hate that man."

"And he knows it. That's probably why he made such a big production of this. How do you suppose he got hold of that information you asked me to keep confidential?"

I thought for a moment. "We're secure here. Mo Rappaport would have no reason to put that in an autopsy report, and I trust him and Earl to keep their mouths shut. I also trust Jackie and David from crime scene, but the sheriff's office is famous for press leaks. I wouldn't trust anyone who types up the crime scene reports. They're all a bunch of political hacks."

"Allan's not shy about paying for information."

"He's a reporter. I trust them as much as lawyers and used car salesmen."

"Hey!"

"You're different."

"Thank you. Can I use any of the secret details you gave me?"

"Go ahead, and use anything you want. Maybe that will stick it up Allan's... Maybe it will make him feel left out when he sees you have more and better information."

Rachel Williamson laughed. "Okay, lover, if you get anything new, call me first."

"You know I will."

Later, Jackie Shuman telephoned.

"I got news, but it ain't good," he said.

"You're a barrel of laughs."

"That anonymous call to 9-1-1 came from a pay phone."

"We still have pay phones?"

"There's a half dozen in the arrivals area at the airport."

"This killer is a clever bastard."

"Don't ask me to look for oil spots in short term parkin'."

"Lazy."

"Catch ya later."

* * * *

We experienced five uneventful days. It still rained off and on, temperatures remained cool and the vegetables refused to grow without sun.

The next day Bettye and I continued to work on the murders and integrate all the daily chores necessary to make a small police department go around.

At one o'clock, just as Bettye was leaving for lunch, I received a phone call from my neighbor and owner of Walking Horse Realty, Glenda Mae Waddell. She was crying, and I knew it was something serious.

"Sam, Lord have mercy," she said. "This is awful. Rosanna was beaten ta death."

And on another sixth day, the killer struck again.

Rosanna Perry had lived in a small pre-World War Two Craftsman catalog home on a cul-de-sac off McTeer's Station Road. The house looked neat, the grounds tidy, and the interior tastefully furnished and spotless.

Rosanna's body lay on the living room floor. A rock, roughly the size of a softball, lay on the carpet next to her damaged skull. The contrast between her platinum blonde hair and the copious amount of cabernet-colored dried blood was startling. Head wounds are always messy.

Jackie Shuman once again handled the evidence collection, this time assisted by a deputy named Neal Brickman. David Sparks had taken the day off. Doctor Morris Rappaport and Earl Ogle were on their knees tending to the body.

"Number six, right?" Morris asked.

I felt embarrassed when I nodded. "Yep."

"Any leads yet?"

"Don't ask."

"Your ship's sinking fast, Samilah."

I shrugged. "At least the Titanic had a band."

He pointed with a latex-gloved hand to his left. "And another biblical message scratched on the coffee table."

"I'll call my friend the priest and see what twenty ten means."

Morris smiled. "I could call a rabbi."

I brought the pathologist up to speed with the tidbit of news Rachel provided. "That bastard Allan Peters called our killer the Angel of the Lord. Mo, if you hear they find that creep strangled, you'll know it was me."

"Oy, reporters. Who would blame you?"

"Excuse me while I get my weekly theology lesson."

I telephoned Declan McGill.

"20:10. And she was killed with a stone," he said. "Your killer knows his Bible, but doesn't go for anything obscure. I'm going to say Leviticus, but hang on while I get you the exact wording."

Computer keys ticked away.

"Okay, ready to copy?" he asked.

"Shoot."

"'The adulterer and the adulteress shall be put to death.'"

"Yikes. It refers to a he *and* a she?" I asked.

"It does."

"And the adulteress would traditionally be stoned to death?"

"She would."

"So I can possibly look forward to the male member of this adulterous duo already being dead or, in the future, getting biblically whacked?"

"It takes two to tango, my friend."

* * * *

Mae Waddell had composed herself and waited for me at the kitchen table, sitting across from PO Bobby John Crockett. She still showed signs of having cried. Her mascara was a little messed up, but as I approached, she smiled at something Bobby said.

Mae is somewhere over fifty. I never asked how far and never ran her name through the driver's license files to get a year of birth. She's blonde, wealthy, can ride a horse as well as a Comanche warrior, and is drop dead gorgeous. I had no doubt Bobby was trying to make time with her, and Mae was flirting right back.

"Mind if I interrupt?" I said.

Mae looked up at me. "Sammy, do you know this young man looks like he could be your son?"

"So people tell me. But I was nowhere near Blount County thirty-three years ago."

"Land's sake, Sammy." Mae feigned a mild case of shock.

Bobby added, "Looks like time for me ta go. See ya, boss." Then he turned on a 500 watt smile. "Bye, Mae."

"You be careful out there, Bobby John." She returned the smile—also high wattage.

I sat in the chair Bobby had used, ready to talk business.

"Tell me about Rosanna Perry."

She waited a long moment to respond. Her eyes clouded, she sniffed and as a tear rolled down the outside of her right cheek, she blotted it with a tissue.

"Sammy, darlin' I've known her for almost ten years."

"I saw her business cards in the other room. She work for you that long?"

"She did. Rosanna was a very good salesperson."

I shifted in my chair. My lower back ached from the dampness, and I couldn't get comfortable.

"What brought you here today," I asked.

"When Rosanna didn't show up in the office this mornin' and didn't answer my calls, I got worried. That was unlike her."

"How did you get into the house?"

"The front door was unlocked."

I frowned. "And you just walked in?" My tone implied I didn't think she did the right thing.

Mae lowered her eyes and looked embarrassed. "Uh-huh." She sounded like a little girl caught misbehaving.

"You should have called 9-1-1 or me first rather than walking into a potentially dangerous situation."

"That's what Bobby John said."

I stared at her and thought that if she arrived a bit earlier we might have had two new bodies.

"Rosanna ever married?"

"Divorced twice."

"Any recent love interests?"

She paused. "More than one, but I don't know if love entered the picture."

"How many?"

"Rosanna was, uh…fond of men."

"What does that mean?" My patience was not limitless.

Mae looked into my eyes and blinked a few times.

"Sammy, let's just say Kate is lucky Rosanna didn't set her sights on you."

"Would you say she was promiscuous?"

"I would say, sugar, she was romantically active."

"With both single and married men?"

"I didn't keep score."

"Mae, your friend was stoned to death. A message the killer left implies she was adulterous. This is no time to protect her reputation. And it's possible a man with whom she was having an affair may be the next victim."

"I understand."

"Did she talk about her liaisons?"

"Nothing and no one specific."

"Should I scrutinize her phone records?"

"I guess."

"Did she look like she was talking to a lover when she made or took calls?"

"Yes."

"Cell phone, landline, and office phone?"

"I only saw her use two of those."

"She have a little black book?"

Mae shrugged. "Look in her purse."

"Or her desk?"

"You're the policeman, and my office is open to you."

A dim bulb flickered in my head.

"You may have just helped me solve six murders."

* * * *

Little black books are, of course, things of the past. Their presence would make life easier for dinosaurs like me, but I had to settle for a smart phone with a whole storage area full of names and phone numbers that Jackie Shuman taught me how to access. Sharp kid that he is, Jackie also knew how to email that alphabetical list to my computer so I could print it out and read it like a normal human being my age.

He also emailed it to Bettye who trusts computers more than I do and wouldn't print it. She would start calling each person on the list and learn what kind of relationship they had with Rosanna Perry. I called Bettye to make sure she knew what I needed.

"Betts, I've got a feeling this is the information we need to get our heads above water."

"I'm glad you're so optimistic."

"Someone—or more than one someone—on that list was having an affair with Rosanna. You find out who, and I may tie him to the killer."

"And just how am I going to do that on the phone?"

"Use your intelligence guided by experience. If someone was secretly getting romantic with Rosanna, he might bob and weave to keep from admitting it. Tell me who you think acted evasive, and I'll talk to them in person. You know I can be persuasive."

"I can just imagine."

"Before you start calling, get as many off-duty guys as you can and send them out to re-canvass the neighborhoods around the other murders. Tell them to look for flies on the wall—the kinds of people we rarely notice because they're always around. Garbage men, phone company employees, cable guys. Have the people they interview focus on actual the times of death we only guessed at before."

"What will you be doin'?"

"I'll hit this neighborhood and see if I can find someone who witnessed something or saw somebody."

"Okey dokey, darlin'. I hope the good citizens of Prospect don't call with too many requests for police service. We'll all be too busy playin' detective."

Ninety percent finished with the area I wanted to cover, my phone sounded off, and my wife reported a minor domestic emergency.

"Sweetie," she said, "the stove died."

"Electric stoves rarely die. Occasionally, they malfunction. What happened?"

"The oven died. Dead. There's no heat."

"Did you check the breakers?"

"How do I do that?"

"The panel in the garage. Look for two switches on the right side labeled range. They're connected and should be pushed to the right like all the others."

"Okay, wait."

"Hang on a minute."

She did.

"Before you go outside, do you get heat from the burners?"

"Yes, all four."

"So the thing is getting juice. Forget the breakers. Is the oven turned off?"

"It is."

"Check the element. See if it's cracked or broken in half or whatever."

"Okay, hang on."

Kate put the phone down and in the background I heard the oven door open. A moment later, she came back.

"You're right. The back of the left side is cracked apart."

"Good. Easy solution."

"Can you pick one up and replace it?"

"Me?"

"Not me."

"I'm scared to death of electricity," I said. "I cringe when I change a light bulb."

"Oh, please."

"Call that little nebbish of a guy who fixes appliances. The guy you share recipes with—Dudley, Digby, Whatshisname."

"Duffy Hines. He'll charge for a service call plus the cost of parts."

"I'd rather pay sixty bucks than get electrocuted."

"But you'd do it so much better, Sammy."

"If you weren't beautiful and sexy, I'd hate you."

"Fat chance."

"Go make a phone call. I've got police work to finish."

* * * *

My neighborhood investigation netted me nothing. So, I drove back to the PD to see how Bettye and the rest of the troops were making out.

"Nobody's called in with excitin' news," she said, "so I assume they haven't learned anythin' new."

"Me either. What have you been doing?"

She sighed and ran a hand through her blonde hair. "Lookin' for those flies. Only Higgins and Quayle and Jane Cousins used landlines in their homes, but all four victim's houses had Charter Cable, and of course all get their power from Alcoa utilities."

"Have you asked if any of the victims have had service calls lately?"

"Waitin' for a call back."

"You might ask if the repair personnel have specific areas of responsibility," I suggested. "These vics may be handled by one cable guy or electrician."

"I'll ask," she said.

"May be nothing. Lots of people want cable TV, and everyone needs electricity."

"You sure know how to rain on someone's parade," she said. "But how about this? Henderson and Cousins owned electric ranges, but the two men and Rosanna Perry had propane and used Foothills Gas to fill their tanks."

"That was good work. I think I love you."

"Thank you, but give it a rest, darlin'."

"We need someone who's around the neighborhoods more often than our cops. Someone who might notice something out of place, an anomaly."

"Like a good fly on the wall," she said.

I nodded. "Too many different places to have the same mail carrier."

"There's got to be someone we're not seeing. I'll think about this."

"Somewhere there's a connection to all the victims," I said. "We'll find it, sooner or later."

"Let's hope it's sooner than later, or someone else may die while we're lookin' for an answer."

"Talk about raining on a parade. You're a real wet blanket."

Bettye tossed her reading glasses onto the desktop and stuck out her tongue at me.

"Is that any way to treat your boss?"

* * * *

I worked on the Rosanna Perry murder for the rest of the day and came up with three possibilities as recent paramours. All were in their forties, had reasonably good jobs, and two were married. I spoke first with the single divorcee, a lizard named Billy Bob Sweet.

He claimed to have met Rosanna at a New Years Eve party. He had no problem telling me they dated off and on, each time ending up in one of their respective beds.

Billy Bob asked, "Who would want to kill her? Rosanna was great in the sack."

If he shed a tear, I guess I missed it.

I met the two married men, Bradley Skinner and Parker Knowles, separately at their offices. Both needed convincing that it was in their best interest to tell me the truth. I wasted a lot of time with that pair before they saw it my way and coughed up a common story. They met Rosanna while house hunting. Rosanna didn't let pesky things like wives deter her romantic pursuits and periodically called the husbands with news of hot new properties and other exciting offers.

Skinner said he and Ms. Perry engaged in no-strings-attached sex several times, but hadn't seen her in months. He could offer no ideas on her killer and didn't seem to share common ground with Rosanna or any other victim.

Parker Knowles appeared to be devastated by losing Rosanna. Their affair lasted, and he had seen her shortly before the murder. Knowles claimed his wife became disinterested in sex while he and Rosanna shared a voracious appetite for it. He admitted the probability of leaving his wife and living with or marrying Rosanna. Other than acting as his therapist for twenty additional minutes, I learned nothing more of investigative value.

All three men looked troubled about the possibility of one of them being the next victim, but no one could think of a dangerous religious fanatic who might be monitoring their lives.

* * * *

I stuck my head out of my office door and growled at Bettye, "You having any luck?"

"Maybe. How 'bout you?"

"Yes and no. You want coffee?"

"Sure. And I've got a doughnut with your name on it."

I brought out two cups filled with fresh coffee and collapsed into a chair next to Bettye's desk. She handed me an old-fashioned jelly doughnut.

"Here ya go, darlin'. Fortify yourself."

I took a bite, followed by a sip and told her about Rosanna Perry's three love interests.

"Busy girl," she said. "Makes you wonder how many more there were."

I shrugged. "What did you learn?"

"I tracked down a driver from the gas company. Remember I said both Higgins and Quayle and Rosanna Perry bought their Propane from Foothills?"

"I do."

"Well, I asked them to search for customers around all our victims, and they found a few more people in those neighborhoods often serviced by the same driver."

"You're a real Sherlock Holmes."

"How about a Sonny Randall?"

"Why do I know that name?"

"She's a detective Robert Parker wrote about."

"Is she blonde, beautiful, and brilliant like you?"

"Thank ya, sir. I believe she is."

"Who's your guy?"

"His name is Anson Toler, and here's what I know about him."

Bettye learned that Toler had been a Sheriff's deputy who, thanks to one hell of a motor vehicle accident found both his legs severely injured. After more than a year of failing to fully recuperate through physical therapy, Toler received a disability pension from the county. To help make ends meet, he took a job filling people's propane tanks. Toler was unmarried and categorized as something of a loner by people at the sheriff's office.

I said, "Let's send someone to pick him up. We need to have a chat."

* * * *

Anson Toler was medium height, husky, and in his late twenties. He shaved his head, wore a close cut mustache and goatee, and his face held the look of a perpetual snit.

When Officer Johnny Rutledge brought him into my office, I offered him a chair, but he remained standing and spoke. "Your man told me you wanted me to help with an investigation. What exactly?"

I explained about the murders and added, "Your route took you near our victims. If I give you dates and times, could you remember seeing anything that might help me?"

A sardonic smile spanned his face. "I haven't been a cop for a few years now, but I didn't forget everything, and I'm not stupid. You expect me to believe that?"

"What do you believe?"

"You're probably trying to pin something on me."

"Have you done *something* I'd be interested in?"

"Nice try." He stuck his hands in his front pockets and shifted impatiently.

"I'm trying to get a little cooperation, and you're playing Joe Paranoid for me."

The sardonic smile came back.

"Okay," I said. "I'll assume your assistance is out of the question. How about I treat you as a suspect? Mind answering a few pointed questions?"

"Yeah, I do mind. Am I under arrest?"

I waited a few seconds to answer. "Not yet."

"Then you can have a car take me back to my job."

I smiled. "Call a taxi."

* * * *

I doubted that Toler could have camouflaged his two-and-a-half ton tanker truck while committing multiple homicides, so I obtained the registration numbers and description of his white Dodge Stratus from the Department of Safety files and sent two cops out to canvas residents in the proximity of the murders to see if the car sounded familiar.

I took Toler's driver's license photo and vehicle information to Rosanna Perry's three ex-lovers. Neither Skinner nor Sweet recognized Anson Toler.

Parker Knowles said, "I recognize him from someplace, but I'm not sure where."

"Does he deliver propane to your house?"

"We have an all electric home."

"Sure you know him and not someone who looks like him? The bald head and goatee are a common style."

Knowles nodded. "It's him. I wish I knew from where."

"Do you know other people who use propane?"

He thought for a moment. "Sure, I guess. But it's not a general topic of conversation. My in-laws do. My father-in-law calls the gas tank his little white submarine."

"Since we first spoke, you've spent time turning this thing over in your mind," I said. "Have you thought of anyone who would kill you because of the affair with Rosanna?"

He shook his head and shrugged at the same time. "If she ever found out, my wife would rather collect alimony than harm me."

"Big life insurance policy?"

"Hundred thousand."

"Not that much nowadays."

Knowles shrugged.

"Someone seems to know about Rosanna's love life and objects to it. You're sure no one knows you had someone on the side?"

"I made sure we were discreet. But who knows? I never met any of Rosanna's previous men friends, but I guess someone might be jealous."

"I think we're looking for somebody more interested in killing you as a moral statement. Jealousy is a great motivator, but none of the other murders looked like it was a key factor."

"That doesn't make me feel any better."

I ended with, "I told the other men the same thing. Keep your eyes

91

open, and don't be afraid to call 9-1-1 if you think something looks dodgy."

* * * *

I arrived home in a downpour that made me wonder if I'd need a rowboat to get to work the next morning. A late model white van with large black lettering that read Hines Appliance Repair sat parked in the gravel turnaround touching the north end of the concrete apron in front of our garage doors. I shut off the Ford and ran between the drops. Standing next to Kate's new Infiniti, I shrugged out of my raincoat and shook off the water.

In the kitchen, I found Kate sitting at the table and a pair of stubby legs protruding from our oven.

"Hi, sweetie," Kate said. "You remember Mr. Hines."

"Sure," I said, "Whaddaya say, Duffy? How's business?"

"Why, hey there, Mr. Jenkins. You doin' all right t'day?"

"A little wet, but I'll live."

Duffy chuckled and emerged from the oven holding the broken element.

"Now right there's yer problem. This sucker costs a hunnert-an'-ten dollars. Them high temper'tures in these self-cleanin' ovens puts a lot o' stress on the heatin' elements."

"Sounds like a rock and a hard place," I said. "Either replace the element or scrub a dirty oven."

"I know you like an electric range, Sammy," Kate said, "but this thing is kind of old. Maybe gas would be a better way to go."

"This thing cost a bundle and probably has lots of life left in it," I said, "Besides, changing over to gas would be a big hassle."

Duffy interjected his expert opinion. "Wouldn't be too bad. There's no natural gas in these parts, but ya could git you a propane set up. Y'all could bring in a line from under yer deck and set up one o' them l'il white submarines out yonder."

Standing up, Duffy Hines looked around three inches shorter than Kate, making the little guy no more than five-four. He was moderately chubby and wore glasses.

"Set up what?" I asked.

"One o' them big propane tanks. They look like a l'il white submarine."

"Do you use propane to cook?"

"Shore do."

"You buy it from Foothills Gas?"

"Yessir. Have done fer years."

I took the photo of Anson Toler from my inside jacket pocket.

"You know this man?"

"Shore. He works fer Foothills Gas. Delivers ta my house. What's he done?"

I opened a drawer, picked up a check book and handed it to Kate.

"Take care of Duffy's bill, please. I've got to make an important phone call."

* * * *

I reached Sergeant Stan Rose while he was parked under the drive-thru of the Prospect Citizen's Bank, staying out of the rain.

"I need you to pick up Anson Toler, the guy I told you about today. The paperwork on him should be on Bettye's desk. Try his home or Foothills Gas if they're working overtime."

"I'll give you a shout when we've got him. What's up?" Stan said.

I explained why I wanted to re-interview Toler.

"It might be tough in this rain," I said, "but check his driveway and see if his private vehicle has an oil leak."

Fifteen minutes later, my cell phone sounded off.

"Toler called in sick today, and he's not at home," Stan said. "A neighbor saw his car earlier this afternoon, but it's gone now."

"How about that oil leak?"

"It's an old car, right? I found spotting under the car port."

"You'd better find him."

"And how's I a'pposed ta do dat, sahib?"

"If I knew, I'd do it myself. You have two patrolmen to help. Use your imagination."

* * * *

I called Parker Knowles, but only spoke to his wife.

"I'm sorry, Chief. Parker had some things he wanted to finish at work. You can find him there."

"What's that phone number again?"

She told me, and I dialed.

"Yes?" he said, sounding odd.

"Mr. Knowles, are you alone?"

"Yes." Again with no inflection.

"Is everything okay? Say something stupid if you can't talk."

"Okay, I'll stop at the store on my way home."

"I'll be right there."

I called Stanley and the other on-duty patrolmen using the car radio.

"Everybody start heading toward Parker Knowles's office at the Admin building next to the Appalachian Vinyl Products warehouse. I think Anson Toler is there."

A moment later, PO Vern Hobbs said, "Cain't be. I got him rot here—Ellejoy Market, corner o' Patterson Road."

* * * *

I told Vern to hang onto Toler until we sorted out the emergency. Stan and PO Bobby Crockett started for Knowles's office building. So did I, and I arrived first with Stanley only moments behind me.

An old Ford Escort station wagon, a dull dark blue and mostly forgettable specimen, sat in a parking space under a tree in a dark corner of the lot. Knowles's black Toyota Avalon was near the door and the only other vehicle present.

I pointed at the Ford. "Who owns that?"

"Beats me," Stan said, "but I'll bet it leaks oil."

"I'm going in. Wait for Bobby, and send him around back before you come in."

Stanley shook his head. "Not your best idea. Watch your ass in there alone."

I nodded, tried the door and found it unlocked. When I entered the small lobby, I shook off some of the rain that covered my coat and drew my Smith and Wesson. A hushed conversation was taking place in one of the rooms down the hall. I moved quietly toward the voices and peeked in when I reached Parker Knowles's office doorway. Knowles sat behind his desk with his palms flat on the blotter. I recognized the man holding a nickel-plated revolver a foot from Knowles's head.

* * * *

Using the door frame to brace my gun, I aimed at Duffy Hines's chest and in a firm, but conversational tone said, "Police, Duffy, don't move."

His eyes flicked toward me, and he froze.

"Very slowly, now," I said. "Lay the gun on the desk."

He hesitated and then tilted his head—like a dog unsure what it just heard.

"Put the gun down. Now." I used a little more emphasis.

It took him a few seconds, but he gently placed an old High Standard Sentinel, a .22 caliber snub-nose, something out of production for almost forty years, on the edge of the desk next to a grapefruit-sized rock. That done, he automatically raised his hands.

The front door opened and closed with a whoosh of the pneumatic arm. Seconds later, Stan Rose stepped up behind me as I walked into the room.

"Call Bobby in from the rain," I said.

Stan depressed the transmit button and spoke into a portable radio.

"Cuff Mr. Hines," I said, still holding my gun in a position to shoot.

The door opened and closed again, and Bobby Crockett stepped into the office holding his Glock with two hands, pointed in a safe direction toward the ceiling.

"Take Mr. Knowles out to your car, Bobby. I want to speak with Duffy before we leave."

Crockett holstered his gun and led the lucky Parker Knowles into the hallway. Stanley stood behind Hines, almost a foot taller than the prisoner.

"Sit down, Duffy," I said.

He took a seat in the big swivel chair and looked like a little boy with a middle-aged face.

"He's your son-in-law, and you found out he was cheating on your daughter." I made it a statement, not a question.

Duffy grinned. "I'm glad ya understand. Adultery is a sin."

95

"Not exactly a capital crime."

He shook his head. "Oh, yes. Says so in the Bible. I believe it, and that's that."

"You were going to stone him to death."

"It's only proper. I mighta shot him, too."

His response made me shrug. "I thought you drove a van."

"I do."

"What's that old rattletrap outside?"

He grinned again. "My fishin' car. Runs good."

His new white van with the repair business information painted on the sides would have drawn attention.

"You take that gun fishing with you?"

"I do. Got it from my daddy. Lemme see. He bought it more'n fifty years ago. Gave it ta me a'fore he died."

An almost dreamy look passed over his face. Duffy Hines seemed calm and contented to sit in the oversized leatherette chair with his hands cuffed behind his back.

"I can understand being pissed off at Parker, but why the others?"

He shook his head and appeared sad. "Then ya don't understand. I thought ya would. Are ya a God-fearing man, Mr. Jenkins?"

In no mood to discuss theological philosophy with a serial killer, I shrugged and said, "Try me."

Duffy sighed, and his shoulders moved up and down two inches. "The good Lord needs workers here on earth—people ta not only spread his word, but ta do his chores. In some cases, avenging angels, ya might say." He ended his thought with a broad smile.

I could hear that bastard Allan Peters' words.

"The things those people done were violations o' God's law," he continued. "Says so in the Scriptures. They's pro-scribed. And the punishments are written for all ta read. I was jest followin' God's laws. Like y'all follows the criminal law." He looked from me to Stanley and smiled again. "The Bible suggests... No. No, it commands what a true believer must do when comin' ta God's aid."

Stan let out a long breath. Our eyes met.

"Each and every time," Duffy said, "I done left ya my justification. Scratched chapter and verse inta somethin' right there. Didn't want

96

nobody thinkin' I was doin' things fer no good reason."

"You repaired appliances at all the victim's homes?"

"More or less. But they ain't victims. They's all sinners."

I blinked a few times. "Duffy, have you got a family lawyer you'd like to call?"

He shook his head and grinned like the village idiot. "Don't need one."

"I think you might."

"Nosir," he said with conviction. "I'll show a judge and jury my Bible. That's all I need. Yessir. That's proof positive."

THE END

Massacre at Big Bear Creek

Wayne Zurl

Acknowledgement

Special thanks to Lonnie MacMillan for my lessons in Smoky Mountain folklore

Massacre at Big Bear Creek
Wayne Zurl

Big Jake MacGregor slammed down the double edged ax and split a red oak log like it was balsa. His older cousin, Andy Hughes, sat on the tailgate of Jake's flatbed pickup, a salt glazed jug of homemade liquor next to his left hand, a Winchester lever action rifle on the right. Andy's face looked like he'd parted company with his razor three days earlier.

Jake's sons, Little Will and Roy "Persimmon Head" MacGregor, walked into the clearing. Three brindle dogs that zigzagged frantically, sniffing the ground, followed them.

Jake hacked a piece off the split log, and Andy took a pull from the jug before they noticed the boys.

A single barrel .20 gauge shotgun dangled from Little Will's right hand, and nineteen-year-old Roy touched the grip of an old Colt revolver tucked into the waistband of his trousers. Both young men were dressed from head to foot in Real-Tree camouflage. Roy looked like he hadn't shaved in two weeks.

Will appeared tired; a serious expression covered his face. "Daddy, we's been down ta Redwine Glade lookin' ta kill that ol' tom turkey who's made that holler his struttin' ground when them dogs found us. They skeered the turkey away."

Andy set the gray jug down on the tailgate. "Yer daddy said them dogs took off on him yesterday when they seen the bear he been trackin.'" His eyes matched the darkest blue of his plaid wool jacket. "You know them ol' Plott dogs will stay with a bear all night an' always come home. Ain't the first time dogs run off a turkey. What's yer point?"

Twenty-one-year-old Will sniffed and wiped his nose with the back of a hand before answering the older man. "Point is, Uncle Andy, I ain't worried 'bout them runnin' off no turkey. I ain't heard them dogs all night. But I did hear a couple shots. If'n they had a bear treed, they woulda kep' on barkin'." He swung the shotgun, let the butt drop to the ground and rested his hands on the muzzle end of the long barrel. Will sighed and attempted to clarify his statement. "Me an' 'Simmon Head, we thought somebody mighta kilt that bear offa our dogs and then whupped them off."

"But looka them dogs," Persimmon Head said. "Ain't nobody whooped them dogs offa no bear. They kilt our bear and blooded them dogs ta chase 'em off."

Jake swung the ax in a short arc, letting the blade cut into his splitting stump and stick there. He whistled twice. "Rusty, git over here, boy."

The oldest of the three dogs broke ranks and hustled over to its master. Jake scratched the Plott hound under the chin and looked the dog over carefully. "Boy's right, Andy. Somebody splattered blood all over this dog."

"Others, too," Roy said, nodding several times.

"You boys find the tree where they kilt that bear?" Jake asked.

"Yessir," Will said, "up ta Welk's Cove, other side o' Harker's Run. They left the carcass an' took the meat an' hide. From the tracks, we figger they's five or six of 'em."

"That ain't far from the campground at Big Bear Creek," Jake said.

"A man could park there and hunt as far as he wanted ta walk," Andy said.

"Cork that jug, Andy," Jake said. "L'il Will, git yerse'f and them dogs inta the truck."

Will opened three of four doors to the cages sitting on the bed of Jake's truck and herded the dogs into their crates.

"'Simmon Head," Jake said, "you got extra shells fer that Colt ya got tucked inta yer britches, son?"

"Yessir, got me a whole pocketful," Roy said.

"Then let's go an' see what we find at the campground. Ain't nobody stealin' my bear."

Jake MacGregor turned his Chevy off the blacktop road that

paralleled Little Slick Rock Creek and headed toward the campground on a single track gravel lane. At the end of the public access road, in a long narrow parking area, he set the shifter in first gear and switched off the ignition. Twenty yards further on, parked on either side of the outhouses supplied by the Tennessee State Parks Department, they found a brown Ford F-150 with a camper cap and Blount County plates on the left and a black four door GMC Sierra with dual rear wheels and North Carolina registration to the right.

Jake grabbed a Marlin .35 caliber carbine from a rack behind the truck seats and exited his vehicle. The two boys and Andy Hughes followed him toward the Ford.

"That's Wicher Kline's truck," Andy said, as he stepped abreast of his cousin. "And looks like Stumpy Nate Laky's with 'im.'"

"I believe so," Jake said."

To their right, almost a hundred feet away, six rough-looking men sat at two picnic tables. A fire burned in one of the stone-sided grills, and two plastic milk jugs filled with moonshine sat on the tables. The smell of barbequed meat hung in the air.

"Wicher, Stumpy Nate," Jake said, "how you boys been?"

Wicher said, "Jake, boys, you doin' aw rot t'day?"

Each man had been eating from bags of jerky and Fritos. Both were approaching middle-age and had dressed warmly for a day of hunting in the shady woods.

Stumpy Nate finished chewing, drank from a tin cup and nodded. "Boys," he said.

The young MacGregors and Andy Hughes nodded back.

Jake tossed a look at the men from North Carolina. "'Pears like they's got lucky huntin'."

"Kilt them a bear not far off," Nate said.

"Now, Stumpy Nate," Andy said, "We believe them boys kilt that bear offa Jake's dogs, and that ain't right."

Nate shrugged. "No, it ain't. We was jest squirrel huntin'. Didn't see no bears."

"Who is that outfit?" Jake asked.

"Don't know no names," Wicher said, "but they's from over Bryson City way."

"They bring that shine with 'em?" Jake asked.

"Nosir," Wicher said. "Ol' Tabcat John Hunnicutt an' Arky Cable come rollin' in here with a truckful on the ways ta Fontana and sold 'em a couple jugs. They offered us some."

"Well," Jake said. "That's my bear, an' I'm gonna talk with 'em 'bout that."

"Whatcha gonna do with them guns, Jake?" Nate asked.

Jake cracked a thin smile. "Might could do a little huntin' after we talk with them boys."

"Now, Jake," Wicher said, "they's been eatin' and a'drinkin' an' carrin' on fer sometime. They's all loosened up like. Don't make no trouble."

"Ain't gonna be no trouble, Wicher. I jest want what's mine." Jake scratched the end of his nose. "But I'm a fair man. They kin have half the meat."

"Jake, I smell a big hoorah comin'. Me an' Stumpy Nate don't want no trouble."

Andy Hughes shifted his Winchester from right hand to left, grasping the forestock. "Then you boys oughta take a ride while we talk this out."

Stumpy Nate nodded and set his cup on the tabletop.

"Give us a minute," Wicher said.

"Jest jump in that truck," Andy said impatiently. "We'll make sure yer gear's safe. Y'all go ahead, and come back in a hour. One of us'll wait fer ya."

As Wicher and Nate drove away, the MacGregor party walked the hundred feet to where the North Carolina group sat.

Big Jake pushed a battered brown fedora back off his forehead, scanned the six men with his eyes and nodded. "Boys, we hear y'all kilt you a bear. I believe it's the one my dogs had treed."

All conversation stopped. Jake MacGregor had made a serious accusation. One man took a sip from a blue and white spatter wear cup he'd been raising to his lips. Other movement ceased. A burly man wearing a red buffalo plaid coat and Mossy Oak camo cap scratched his dark beard. "What makes ya think it's yer bear?"

"Found the carcass nearby. Looked like six men drug the meat this way," Andy said. "Ain't really no other place ta come an' find a parked truck."

"I appreciate the fact ya didn't whup my dogs," Jake said. "But ya blooded 'em ta run 'em off. And that's my bear."

The bearded man shook his head. "Your opinion."

"I ain't tryin' ta be unreasonable an' don't want no trouble," Jake said. "You kilt that bear and cut it up. Lotsa work there, so yer entitled to somethin'. But I want half the meat…and the hide. Was my dogs who treed that bear. You ain't got no dogs with ya."

"Half the meat is reasonable." The man nodded for a long moment. "But we done butchered it, we carried it, and that hide is worth cash money. I don't think so."

Jake made eye contact with Andy and then looked back at the bearded man. "Don't want no trouble, boys, but fair's fair."

Andy raised his rifle to hip level and pointed it at the bearded man. Little Will and Persimmon Head tensed up and exchanged glances. The North Carolina crew began to look worried.

"We'll jest take half that meat *and* the hide and be on our way," Jake said. "That way, y'all kin git back ta yer likker."

The bearded man shook his head." Nosir. Cain't give ya the hide. We don't want no trouble, neither, but that's the way it is."

Andy cocked the hammer on his old '94 Winchester, adjusted his point of aim an inch and squeezed the trigger. As the bearded man grasped his chest and blood oozed through his fingers, Andy worked the lever, racked a fresh 38-55 round into the chamber and shot another man in the forehead. In a split second, he did the same thing a third time.

After Andy's first shot, Persimmon Head drew the Colt Trooper from his waistband and shot one man. He fired four rounds; two bullets struck his victim in the chest. Little Will leveled his shotgun and slapped the trigger, hitting one man with the majority of pellets while a few others struck another man on his left. Big Jake raised the Marlin carbine to his shoulder and killed the man Little Will wounded. Everything happened in only a matter of seconds.

Jake's dogs began to bark and howl when the gunfire started and continued as the smoke settled.

"Whoo-ee," Persimmon Head said, with inappropriate glee. "Lord have mercy. I ain't never seen a man shoot faster, Uncle Andy."

"Shut up, "Simmon Head," Will said.

"Shut up them dogs, Will," Jake yelled. The boy knew his father was angry.

"That ol' boy made a move," Andy said, defensively. "Figgered he was makin' a play fer his gun." He looked from Jake to the boys. "And I didn't want none o' the others ta draw down on us. Y'alls did the rot thing."

"Don't see no guns at hand, Andy," Jake said. "I believe we're gonna have trouble over this."

* * * *

The TWRA, Tennessee Wildlife Resources Agency, officers called Prospect PD after they found the bodies a few yards off the Panther Fork Road in Orr's Valley. Six corpses had been unceremoniously dumped less than twenty feet off the blacktop. The wildlife officers found a black, heavy-duty GMC pickup driven deep into a thicket three hundred yards up the road.

An officer named Gary Carver said, "We didn't touch anythin'. Except ta check for vital signs."

He went on to explain how each man had been killed. Carver and his partner were dressed in forest green fatigues and wore short matching jackets.

"Y'all can see for yase'f a shotgun and at least one other gun was used," Wildlife Officer Ed Finch said. "But we don't figure only two people could shoot six men up front with none o' them tryin' to run away. Must have been a larger group o' shooters."

I nodded. "You get any ID on these men?"

"Wasn't a robbery," Carver said. "They all had wallets, and their guns were in the pickup. Four from Bryson City and two from Birdtown, a little place between there and Cherokee."

"You contact the families?" I asked.

"North Carolina State Police did. Best they can figure, this bunch came here ta hunt four days ago."

"They into anything that could get them killed?"

"Not that we know," Finch said.

"If they were here four days, where do you suppose they camped?"

"Big Bear Creek Campground isn't far off. That's the only place with facilities. Course, they could make a crude camp in any glen or holler they took a fancy to."

The sun was shining, but the breeze had picked up, and in the shade it seemed colder than the forty-five degrees that had shown on the dashboard thermometer of my unmarked Crown Victoria when I arrived. I tipped up the collar of my jacket and gave an involuntary shiver as I scanned the area.

"Wonder why they dumped the bodies and then moved the truck? Kinda risky," I said.

"Here's easier for the animals ta get ta the bodies," Carver said. "Then there goes your evidence. Not much risk, though. This road ain't used much. The hills are too steep for hunters."

"And no one lives anywhere close."

He nodded.

"Makes me think the killers were hunters," I said.

"Everybody around here are hunters," Finch said.

I nodded. "Pardon me. I'm just a city boy."

They laughed.

"While I'm waiting for the ME and crime scene guys, can you hit the campground and see if there's anything there worth knowing?"

Both officers nodded. To a casual observer, we might have looked like three big Bobble-Heads.

"Treat the place as part of the crime scene until we know differently," I said. "Look for some of their gear. Pay attention to tire tracks. Anything might be important. And if they were killed there, you'll see plenty of blood."

Finch nodded again.

Carver said, "You got it, Chief."

The wildlife officers drove off, and I walked around the scene where the bodies had been dropped. A rookie detective could have deduced that everyone had been killed elsewhere and the bodies moved to where shortly a small army of police officers would comb the woods for clues.

PO Vernon Hobbs, the guy I call the shortest cop on earth, walked over.

"Looks like the results of a feud," he said, and shifted a toothpick from one side of his mouth to the other.

"Like the Hatfields and McCoys."

"They's up in Kentucky and thereabouts."

"But these North Carolina boys are in our backyard." I shook my head. "You've been here since before Davy Crockett was born. Know any locals who had a grudge against this bunch?"

Vern is over sixty and didn't take offense at my reference to age.

"Not off hand. Never seen nobody from this outfit b'fore. Know anything about 'em?"

"North Carolina state cops called the families for TWRA. I know where they're from, but nothing else."

Vern did the toothpick thing again. "Well, a'fore too long, ya need ta talk with LeRoy McMurray. He knows all the dirt 'bout these mountain folk."

* * * *

I sat in my car waiting for reinforcements when Gary Carver called my cell phone.

"Big Bear Creek Campground's the place ya need ta be. Looks like that North Carolina crew got shot while they were sittin' at a couple o' picnic tables. Bunch o' gear scattered around, and somebody used a tree branch ta cover their tracks. Ya might get another crime scene unit over here."

Six murders would qualify as a bona fide massacre to the Knoxville press and TV newscasters. Before the first forensic workers arrived in Orr's Valley, television news aircraft did flyovers to get a glimpse of the action. A traffic reporter's single engine airplane made several passes up and down the valley, while a chopper hovered above our three police cars.

Shortly after Deputy Medical Examiner Morris Rappaport and his assistant Earl Ogle arrived, a second morgue wagon pulled in to accommodate the extra bodies. They were followed by two crime scene units from the county sheriff's office, a heavy-duty wrecker and a bus with thirty recruits from the county police academy, sent to assist in scouring the woodland for physical evidence. Interspersed among the official personnel, newspaper reporters, photographers, and TV personalities with their cameramen began arriving. I used POs Vern Hobbs and Johnny Rutledge to keep the vultures from harassing the workers.

"I guess someone thought they had a good reason to kill six people," Morris said.

"Or they're just goddamned evil," I suggested.

The doctor bent over a large bearded man wearing a blood-soaked red and black plaid coat. "This one took a single shot to the heart. The two I looked at with head shots had the backs of their skulls blown off as the bullets exited. From the looks of the entry wounds, this trio was shot with a similar caliber. Looks like a .38 or 9mm."

"The guy in the field jacket Earl is working on has two .38-sized holes in his chest," I said. "But they look a little different. Probably copper jacketed rather than lead. These are cleaner holes, maybe semi-wadcutter, and it had to be a heavier bullet and pretty hot load to blow up a skull like that."

"I'll let you know what I dig out of his chest," Morris said.

"Ask Earl to hand carry the bullets to Bill Werner at TBI. He's the best firearms examiner around. I need something to match with any guns I end up confiscating."

"You sound optimistic, Samilah."

By calling me Samilah, Mo's Yiddish name for me, he never lets me forget I'd been born in Brooklyn.

I shook my head. "Why should I be gloomy? It's not like I've got six bodies out in the middle of nowhere."

* * * *

The next day, I sat in my office at Prospect PD with my head spinning as I tried to sort out all the evidence collected at the murder scene and spots where the bodies and truck had been dumped. Back in New York, where I worked for twenty years, we'd utilize two teams of detectives to investigate a massacre like this. In Tennessee, I could turn the case over to the county detectives or the Tennessee Bureau of Investigation or handle it myself, stealing a few of my patrol officers from their normal duties to help out. My ego didn't allow me to kiss this off to someone else, so I muddled through more physical evidence than I could shake a 'possum at and waited for the reports and photographs to come in. Then my phone rang.

"I've got the results on the ammunition from your murders," Bill Werner said.

"That was quick. You're a good man, Willie."

"I hope you remember that the next time you're in Knoxville having lunch at Chesapeake's."

It wasn't exactly a subtle hint.

"I certainly will. I've always said you're good company."

He chuckled. "I can't hand you a bunch of killers on a platter, but I had luck with what the good doctor sent me."

"I'm listening."

"Let's take the shotgun first. It killed one and wounded another. Copper-plated number six shot. Beyond that, I'm guessing. Might be something a turkey hunter would use. From the number of pellets recovered, I'll say a .20 gauge fired through a full choke barrel."

"A lot of mountain folk use a .20 gauge," I offered.

"Then there are two handgun rounds. 158 grain copper jacketed .38 special. Old-fashioned stuff. Probably surplus ammo bought at a gun show. From the twist, I'd say a Colt with a six inch barrel."

"Could be a .38 or a .357," I said.

"The gun could, but the round was a .38. Don't know of anyone who makes or made a magnum with old-style round nose 158s. Course, someone could load his own."

"You start looking for matches from other shootings yet?"

"You think you're dealing with an amateur?"

"Not me." I laughed. "Dreadfully sorry, old son."

"Okay. Now we get to the rifles. The guy with the turkey shot in his shoulder was killed by a .35 Remington semi-jacketed round. Most common modern gun in that caliber is a Marlin 336. Unfortunately, they're sold in every gun shop, Kmart and Walmart in the country."

"Lucky me."

"Then we get more interesting. An oldie but goodie. At first glance, someone might assume the bullets that went into one man's chest and what the doctor says went through two men's heads were a typical .38.

Well, technically it is a .38, but it measures .379, not .357. So, it didn't come from a .38 or .357 magnum cartridge. It's a heavy bullet, 265 grains of lead that probably began life as a flat nose. A couple makers manufacture something like that."

"38-55?" I asked.

"You know your old guns. The rifling suggests Winchester. That would make it a model 1894. But it's old, pre-1940. A good caliber. The bear hunters love it."

* * * *

Shortly after I hung up on Bill Werner, crime scene investigator Jackie Shuman walked in and dropped two thick manila envelopes on my desk.

"Thanks fer callin' us in on that one, Sam. I'll be able ta put my first born through college on the overtime I made out there."

"Beside taxpayer's cash, what did you guys get?"

"Those killers thought they was slick usin' brush ta clean up their tracks, but they didn't git everythin'. Someone musta used one o' the outhouses and left a footprint in the dirt. A chunk o' heel was cut off and that makes a unique impression. Won't be no doubt if you find me a boot."

"Sounds good. What else?"

"Musta thought they wouldn't leave no tire marks in the gravel road, but they overlooked a spot where the bluestone meets the blacktop. Park maintenance people filled in a low spot with dirt b'fore they dumped more gravel. Looks like a pickup or SUV made a right turn headin' away from the dump site towards Rawlin's Holler, 'tween Painter Mountain and Morton's Knob."

"Even better. Any more?"

"One o' the cups they's usin' had enough moonshine left in it ta analyze. Might be he'pful, might not. David took it over ta Bat Masterson at the TBI Lab. Said he'd call ya t'day, soon as he knew somethin'."

"Bear hunters, moonshine and places called Panther Mountain and Morton's Knob." I shook my head. "Sounds like a far cry from the stuff I dealt with in New York."

Jackie laughed. "I suspect so. Welcome ta the Smokies."

"What do you think of Vern's theory that this could be a feud?"

"Ya mean like moonshiners fightin' fer territory?"

"Or something like a simple hunter's turf war or old-timey family feud or hell, I don't know."

"Could be anythin', I s'pose. You need ta talk with Ol' Mrs. Sparks, David's great mamaw and Will's great great aunt. She's been livin' in these parts longer than anyone I know. Course, she's ninety somethin' and maybe ain't hittin' on all eight cylinders no more." Jackie snapped his fingers. "Hold on, now. There's a feller who might know jest as much. Man name o' LeRoy McMurray knows all the history o' the people in that part o' Prospect."

"That's the second time he's been mentioned. What's his story?"

"LeRoy's a storyteller. Goes out huntin' with all them ol' boys and talks ta the locals and ol' folk collectin' information. He gits paid ta tell Smoky Mountain folklore stories at festivals and such."

"Where can I find LeRoy?"

* * * *

After Jackie left, I drove to the Shrimp Shack, a seafood market and restaurant owned by two Cajun brothers who ended up in Prospect after being dispossessed by Hurricane Katrina. I ordered an oyster poor boy and a pint of Blue Tick English Bitters made at a new brewery in nearby Maryville. As someone called my name at the pickup counter, my cell phone rang. TBI Agent Rodney "Bat" Masterson was calling with his lab results.

I carried the sandwich platter back to my table and spoke into the phone. "Whatcha got for me, cowboy?"

"Will you stop that? I'm from Rhode Island. I've never been to Dodge City and do not have a famous ancestor."

"Okay. Tell me what you know while I eat my oysters."

"Oysters? I've got peanut butter and jelly on whole wheat in a wrinkled brown bag, and you're eating oysters?"

"Did I mention the pint of micro-brewed English Bitters?"

"Jeez!"

"Come to Prospect someday, and I'll buy you lunch."

"Deal. Now, let's talk moonshine."

I cradled the phone against my ear, took a bite of poor boy and mumbled something.

"That was top quality liquor you found," he said. "Best I've seen since Popcorn Sutton was in business."

"Wow. I remember him. Good stuff, huh?"

"Cut to about a hundred proof, but damn near perfect booze."

"*Cut* to a hundred proof? Yikes."

"Yeah, some of that shine goes out at one-ninety—that's ninety-five percent pure alcohol. Burns blue and can knock your socks off with one drink."

"I'm impressed. How do I find out who distills this world-class hooch?"

"I called a friend at the TABC. He said he'd lend a hand. Give him a call."

I dug out a pen, ripped a paper towel from the roll sitting on my table and began writing. "Okay, Tennessee Alcoholic Beverage Commission. I'm ready to copy."

He gave me a Knoxville phone number.

"And his name is?"

"Special Agent Buster Ness."

I laughed. "A revenuer named Ness. You're kidding."

"Nope. And he has no famous ancestors either. You'll like him. Buster's a good ol' boy who's been doing this for more than thirty years. And he's got a good-looking partner, too. Think Jamie Lee Curtis with long hair."

"I can hardly wait."

* * * *

I spent the rest of my day preparing a case against the killers. Unfortunately, the best I could do was pencil in John Does as my suspects.

The next morning I headed north and found the TABC offices at 4420 Whittle Springs Road, south of I-640 and east of Broadway in North Knoxville.

A receptionist handed me a visitor's pass to wear and pointed me in the direction of the Special Investigations Unit. I knocked on the jamb of an open door and was greeted by a big gray-haired, red-faced guy sitting at one of the two desks in the room. I introduced myself, and he reciprocated.

"Buford Ness," he said." But ever'body calls me Buster. Good ta meet ya."

"Same here," I said. "Think you can teach me all about moonshine in one morning?"

He laughed. "Sure. Only drink the good stuff and ya won't go blind."

As Buster continued to laugh, a tall enchanting creature, hovering around fifty, with wavy red hair, walked in carrying a few file folders.

"This here's my partner, Lily Melrose," Buster said.

She stuck out a right hand for me to shake, and I noticed rings on her pinkie and index finger.

"Hi, Sam Jenkins from Prospect PD."

Lily smiled and looked a lot like Jamie Lee Curtis. "Ah, the guy with the six murders to investigate."

"That's me."

Buster said, "Sam wants us to he'p him out with the moonshine he's got in evidence."

"We can try." She spoke with only a hint of a Smoky Mountain accent. I thought she worked hard at disguising it.

"Rod Masterson says the untaxed liquor we found looked like some of the best he's ever seen. He suggested you'd know who was cooking up the good stuff down in my area."

Lily dropped the folders on her desk, sat in a low back swivel chair and crossed a pair of great legs.

"Compared to years ago," she said, "there are relatively few fulltime moonshiners in the Smokies. As you probably know, marijuana became the cash crop of choice with the local miscreants. I don't even want to start discussing meth cookers."

"If y'all found a sample of some really fine stuff like Bat tol' me about," Buster said, "and ya think it originated in Prospect or thereabouts, I'm guessin' it came from ol' Tabcat Hunnicutt. He's been in yer neck o' the woods fer years, but sells his shine all over east Tennessee, southeast Kentucky and inta North Carolina. He's got a big sales network."

I'd heard stories about how difficult it was to put the still operators out of business, and quite frankly, I didn't care enough about untaxed whiskey to invest the time and manpower to track down clandestine distillers in the hills of Prospect.

"Does Tabcat have any regular employees I should know about?" I asked.

"Probably a dozen locals who might show up occasionally when he needs help," Lily said, "but one good ol' boy seems to be his faithful sidekick. Look for a little troll named Arky Cable. He's the full timer who helps Tabcat John run the illegal liquor to his customers."

I jotted down more information and we chatted for another thirty minutes before I headed back to Prospect.

* * * *

Vern Hobbs and I drove to a place called Burchfield Bottoms looking for our pair of moonshiners. At the Hunnicutt homestead, a woman named Patsy told us Tabcat John had taken a drive across the national park to visit a friend in Cosby, but we might find Arky Cable at home down the road a'piece. Ten minutes later, we did. Arky Cable was a wizened little specimen around sixty that looked no more than a hundred-and-twenty pounds soaking wet. We found him feeding a couple of chickens behind his small stick framed house. Twenty minutes later, and we all sat in the squad room at Prospect PD.

"I guess you heard about the six murders at Big Bear Creek Campground," I said.

"Yessir," he said, sitting back in a metal side chair with his legs crossed. "Shame them boys died, but God works in mysterious ways, don't he?"

I smacked him on the side of the head and grabbed his right boot. As I suspected, the heel had been cut partially off by a sharp rock and undoubtedly matched the shoe impression Jackie Shuman found.

"You and Tabcat John sold the dead men liquor," I said. "As far as I know, you were the last people to see them alive. Maybe you killed them and took their money and other property."

"Me?" he croaked. "I ain't never kilt nobody and never stold nuthin'.”

“Arky,” Vern said, “How long we knowed each other?”

“Don’t know, Vernon. All our lives, I suspect. We growed up t’gether.”

“Then, Arky, I’ll tell ya like a friend. Don’t lie ta this man. He’s got him a way ta see through ya. And if he thinks yer lyin’, he’ll beat the fool outta ya ‘til yer blood’s gone. He kin be mean and hateful when he wants ta.”

Arky looked at Vern and then me. “Ain’t no reason ta be hateful, sir. I ain’t lied ta ya. Don’t know nuthin’ ‘bout them killin’s.”

I slapped him again, not hard enough to hurt, but I wanted him to feel like a naughty child. “You know what you saw at Big Bear Creek.” I figured he could ID other people and needed a little more persuasion. I cocked my hand for another shot. “Who else was there?”

He flinched. “Don’t hit me again. Please. I ain’t tryin’ ta deceive ya. Me and Tabcat John, we jest sold them boys two jugs o’ likker. Arrest me fer that, but not for no murder.”

“Arky,” Vern said, “don’t play games with this man. He’ll beat ya more senseless then ya already are and then lock ya in a cell ‘til the rats eat ya ears off. Who else was at Big Bear when ya sold them North Carolina boys the likker?”

Arky Cable hung his grizzled head. “Aw rot, Vernon, I jest don’t want no trouble. Ol’ Wicher Kline and Stumpy Nate Laky was there eatin’ somethin’ afore they went back ta more squirrel huntin’.”

“They drinkin’ likker?”

“Nosir, we offered ‘em some, but they didn’t buy none.”

“Those two having trouble with the North Carolina crew?” I asked.

Arky shook his head. “Stumpy Nate and Wicher don’t got trouble with nobody.”

“So what happened?”

“Nuthin’. That’s what I’s been sayin’. We sold them boys the moonshine and took off headin’ towards Fontana.”

We let Arky Cable go and focused on finding Wicher Kline and Nate Laky. I walked around feeling pleased about the valuable information I’d gotten until I learned that pair seemed to have dropped off the edge of the planet—until a day later when two coon hunters found a body at a place called Slippery Ford along Sharpe's Creek.

Wicher Kline lay face down on the forest floor, three feet from a babbling stream. An old Winchester pump shotgun stood upright propped against an oak tree only two yards away. A single bullet hole between his shoulder blades ruined his rust brown Carhartt jacket.

The next morning, after an autopsy, Dr. Morris Rappaport told me about the 265 grain lead bullet he dug out of Wicher's back that measured .379 of an inch.

My first thought: Same killer. The second: Stumpy Nate was living on borrowed time, or he was already dead.

* * * *

I found LeRoy McMurray standing next to a short bed Ford Pickup as red as his wind burned cheeks. He stood about five-ten, was stocky but not fat, and wore a set of blue denim Liberty Brand overalls and a plaid woolen shirt. A sweat stained, light brown fedora sat on his head above a short reddish brown beard, liberally sprinkled with gray.

Before I met LeRoy, I learned that he was sixty-four and had retired from a long term job with the Aluminum Company of America to make a cottage industry from storytelling, making hollow-wing-bone and short-box turkey calls and primitive knives at the portable forge he kept in the shed next to his home in Happy Valley.

"Mr. McMurray, I'm Sam Jenkins from Prospect PD."

We shook hands.

"Good ta meetcha. Call me LeRoy."

"Okay, LeRoy. You call me Sam,"

He nodded. "My pleasure."

He slammed the tailgate on his pickup. An expensive-looking stainless steel, two place dog cage took up most of the four-by-six-foot truck bed.

"What kind of dogs do you have?" I asked.

"Jest a couple o' ol' mountain curs. Good huntin' dogs, though. Them ol' boys'll chase anythin' from a l'il squirrel to a four hunnerd pound bear."

"Been hunting long?"

"All my life. Kilt my first bear when I's fourteen."

"I'm told you're the guy who knows more about the people and folklore of this area than anyone else."

He shrugged. "Well, I don't know about that, but I talk a lot and hear a lot from the folks 'round these parts."

"You mind helping me solve the recent murders that took place in the hills around Prospect?"

"Don't know no more than what I seen on the news."

"But maybe you can steer me in a direction that can help. Got a few minutes to talk?"

He nodded. "We can. It ain't too bad out today. Wanna set on the porch?"

"Sounds good."

We walked a few feet and climbed four wooden steps to a porch that spanned the entire front of his house. He pointed me to an old-fashioned rocking chair, and he sat in the twin.

"Ain't got no likker, but kin I git ya somethin' ta drink?"

LeRoy had a delivery and voice that would make an actor weep with jealousy.

"No thanks. I'm good."

Neither the local boys who worked for me nor I had much luck getting the residents of the backwoods sections of Prospect to offer any help finding the killers of the six North Carolina men. One woman put it plainly when she said, "They's outsiders an' hits none o' our bidness what happened ta them on our side o' the mountains."

I needed to hook LeRoy's interest and compassion to gain his trust and assistance.

"Everyone's heard about the six men killed at Big Bear Creek," I said. "But maybe you haven't heard about the local man they found murdered at a place called Slippery Ford—nice man named Wicher Kline."

"I did hear, this mornin' on the TV. Yer right, Wicher was a good man. I've knowed him a long time."

"And no one seems to know why somebody would kill him—except me."

That turned his poker face into a quizzical expression.

"I think Wicher witnessed the massacre of those North Carolina boys or he knew who did it."

"Lord have mercy." LeRoy shook his head. "Cain't imagine what his wife'll do without 'im."

"I spoke with her, and she's quite distraught." I paused and shook my head. "A man shouldn't die for no good reason." Then, keeping up my theatrical act, I waited a long moment before dropping my next bomb. "And I think Wicher's friend Nate Laky might already be dead, or he's the next one on the killer's list."

LeRoy seemed pretty good at controlling his emotions, but when he heard that, he waivered. "Stumpy Nate?"

"I can't find him, and no one else knows where he might be."

"Stumpy Nate's divorced and lives alone."

"I know. I heard his sister lived with the horseman who owns Tuckaleechee Stables, but he says she left him almost a year ago. She's dropped off the radar, too. And I figure she might know where to find Nate."

McMurray spent a moment nodding. "Her name's Willa Jean. Heard she married a half-breed name o' Harr'd Kupper." I interpreted that to mean Howard Cooper. "He works at the casino in Cherokee. Must live somewhere on the reservation or thereabouts."

Moderate success. "Thanks. Mind a few more questions?"

He rocked back and forth a few times. "Nosir."

"I'd like to give you some information we never released to the press. Can I trust you to never repeat it…to anyone?"

He nodded. "I kin keep a secret if'n I have ta."

"They used a few different guns to kill the North Carolina men, a shotgun and two common caliber guns, but the one responsible for taking out three at Big Bear Creek *and* Wicher Kline came from a Winchester 38-55—not a rifle you often see anymore."

LeRoy's eyes narrowed, and he squinted at me silently.

"Know any hunters in the neighborhood who uses one of those? Probably a model '94."

He adjusted his hat and sighed before answering. "I do. Now, I cain't prove none o' what I tell ya, but…"

"Not your job to prove anything, LeRoy. That's why they pay me a meager salary. Just give me a hint so I can look elsewhere."

"Ever hear 'bout a man named Andy Hughes?"

"No."

"Andy, he's kinda famous around these parts. Actually, I should say notorious. People think he's sorta crazy. Might could kill ya as quick as look at ya. Word is he already kilt three, maybe four people."

"He ever arrested?"

"Couple times fer runnin' moonshine. But people thought his white dog was so bad, nobody'll buy from 'im no more. Called it rotten likker, they did. Then he got caught poachin' deer and once fer stealin' a car when he's young. Believe he did some jail time fer that."

"How about these alleged murders?"

"Might be jest talk, but probably not. I know two stories. One about this ol' boy he shot fer makin' advances on his wife. Other 'bout a young'un he thought kilt his dog. Shot'em both in the back."

"You believe the stories?"

He nodded slowly. "I do. Ain't ever seen Andy he wasn't holdin' his long barreled Winchester. Carries a .45 Colt pistol sometimes, too."

"He work?"

"Drives a gravel truck sometimes fer Tater Russell over in Townsend, cuts far wood, does some bush hawgin', this and that work."

"Who does he hang out with?"

"Mostly keeps ta himse'f, but when he does keep company, he runs with his cousins, Big Jake MacGregor and his boys."

"He hunts with the MacGregors?"

"Yessir."

"Where can I find them?

"That whole MacGregor tribe lives over ta Orr's Valley. Jake got him a shop where he does small engine repair out front o' his house. Ya cain't miss it."

"Where does Andy live?"

"Ya go east o' Jake's 'bout a quarter mile and take the road that goes through the valley and then veers off and dead ends at the base o' Painter Mountain."

"Thanks, LeRoy." I stood up, ready to leave.

"I'd 'preciate it if ya didn't mention where ya got this information."

I grinned. "What information?"

He smiled, and we shook hands.

"Good ta meet ya," he said.

* * * *

Howard Cooper was a big, dark haired man who worked security at Harrah's casino on the Cherokee reservation. He told me I'd find his new wife, Willa Jean, working in the gift shop at the Oconoluftee Cherokee Museum.

Only five minutes of conversation with Willa Jean convinced her that brother Stumpy Nate was in danger. She arranged to take personal time off and handle a family emergency.

In the living room of her small house, off US-19 halfway between Cherokee and Waynesville, we found Brother Nate holding a single barrel .12 gauge, pointed roughly at my head.

Nate was shorter than his older sister and deserved the name stumpy. He was dressed in a red flannel shirt and baggy carpenter's jeans. He looked like a Smoky Mountain Hobbit.

"Whatsa matter with ol' Andy Hughes?" he asked. "He need ta hire him a hit man ta keep me quiet?"

Nate cocked the shotgun's exposed hammer, and Willa Jean screamed, "Lord have mercy, Nathan, he's a po-leeceman."

For some reason, she needed to shuck off a quilted jacket and drop it on the floor. It felt warm in the house, but I wasn't having a hot flash.

"Shore he is," Nate said sarcastically. "Don't be stupid, Willa Jean. Andy wants me an' Wicher Kline dead, and he sent this gunman ta find me."

Normally a shotgun staring at my nose would get me unglued, but I doubted Stumpy Nate would have splattered my brains against the Nuevo Native American artwork on the wall behind where Willa Jean and I stood.

"For chrissakes, Stumpy Nate," I said. "I'm the chief at Prospect PD. My badge is in my right pocket. I'll show you."

"Ya cain't fool me, mister. Anybody kin git hisse'f a fake badge."

I really wanted to smack the little bastard. "Then I'll show you my photo ID along with a driver's license and a half dozen credit cards. Goddamnit, don't I look at a cop?"

A long moment passed before Nate chose to speak.

"Aw rot," he said, squinting down the barrel. "Nice an' slow like, take yer wallet out an' give it ta Willa Jean."

I did and in only scant moments we established I wasn't a button man for the hillbilly mafia.

"Last I seen," Stumpy Nate said, "was Andy Hughes tellin' me an' ol' Wicher Kline ta take a ride outta the campground while him an' Big Jake an' them MacGregor boys talked things over with that outfit from Bryson City. An hour or so later, me an' Wicher, we come back ta Big Bear and the stupid one 'Simmon Head's a'waitin' fer us. Ain't no one else around. He says Big Jake straightened things out an' he gives us one o' the jugs o' Tabcat John's likker. Said hit was part o' the deal fer the bear meat."

"That's it?" I asked.

"I didn't like the smell o' that, but what's we supposed ta do?"

I couldn't watch over Stumpy Nate in North Carolina, so he accepted my offer of protective custody in Blount County, Tennessee. We jumped into my car, took US-441 over the 6,643 foot mountain, Clingman's Dome, through New Found Gap, then along the river on the national park road and back to familiar territory.

In a seldom seen display of affection for me, Chief Assistant District Attorney Moira Menzies offered to complete the material witness paperwork and arranged for two of the DA's investigators to meet me and Stumpy Nate at a motel near the airport in Alcoa. She promised that her minions would keep the Stumpster safe until I collared Andy Hughes and selected members of the clan MacGregor. People tend to bend over backwards for the guy who clears seven homicides in one day.

* * * *

Sergeants Bettye Lambert and Stan Rose sat in the guest chairs in front of my desk, Bettye with her left leg crossed over the right and Stanley with his long legs stretched to the front. POs Junior Huskey and Bobby John Crockett leaned against the wall to the left of my door and my department sharpshooters, Vernon Hobbs and Harlan Flatt, stood in front of the windows facing the lobby.

"It looks like we'll be dealing with four people," I said. "Unless any friends or family want to help them resist arrest."

"What do you think about that, Vern," Bettye asked.

"If them Bryson City boys was the only ones kilt, mebbe. But I'm guessin' everybody knows Andy Hughes done shot Wicher Kline. Wicher's one o' their own. Ain't nobody gonna miss Andy if he goes ta jail."

He took a minute to look around the room and mess with his toothpick. "Them MacGregors ain't no bad apples. Young 'Simmon Head's a might slow, mebbe even stupid-like, but I doubt they'll give us any trouble."

"Be safer if we popped them one at a time," I said. "Having allies standing next to you often builds false courage."

"What ya say's true, Sam," Vern said, "but ya arrest one and word'll spread like wildfire, and the other three will hightail it outta town."

"This is beginning to sound like the Old West," Stanley said.

"Okay," I said. "Any ideas on how we get all four together at the same time without waiting for Thanksgiving dinner?"

"Tommorrow's November 11th, Armistice Day," Vern said. "Weather's s'posed ta be in the sixties and clear. Nobody'll be workin', so I suspect they'll all be over ta Melody Springs picnic area. Each year they hold a little heehaw a'fore winter. They'll be eatin' and dancin' and socializin'. Toby Runyan'll bring his banjo, and ol' Harvey Proctor'll play the fiddle. Might be some likker, so best we git there early a'fore they loosen up too much."

"I think six of us can handle this," I said and looked at the five men present. "If the balloon goes up, Bettye can send in the cavalry. I'll call TWRA and see if Carver and Finch can be there, too."

"Ya want some heavy weapons?" Harley asked.

I nodded. "Bring your AR-15. Vern, bring your rifle. Big guns tend to give us a psychological advantage. You can hang back and watch the crowd. The four of us will take the prisoners. Sound okay?"

Everyone nodded.

"Good. We can kick this around more tomorrow morning, but if there's nothing else, we'll leave here at noon and get there before the liquor starts flowing."

123

"High noon," Stanley said. "How symbolic."

* * * *

The city of Prospect maintained the picnic area called Melody Springs. A naturally flowing spring formed the headwaters of Melody Branch, a gurgling stream that's smaller than a run or brook and feeds into the much larger Big Bear Creek. Engineers excavated a U-shaped clearing, and the city council provided tables, grills, two rather civilized-looking comfort stations and a long, shallow gravel parking area.

A blacktop road formed one boundary where I arranged to have Wildlife Officers Carver and Finch sit in their four-wheel-drive pickup, while the Prospect cops and I went in to make the arrests. A steep hill and Melody Branch blocked the rear of the picnic grounds, and a thicket called a laurel slick by the locals kept each side almost impenetrable. If Stanley was still thinking Old West, he might have called this a box canyon.

As we drove into the parking lot, the musicians were playing a Smoky Mountain version of a Scottish reel. Three couples were dancing, while most people just sat around tapping a foot.

I spotted a place where three tables had been pulled together end to end. A tall heavyset man wearing a fedora and an open flannel shirt over his denim overalls stood talking with two women. At the opposite end, an older and thinner man sat with a rifle-length Winchester propped against the edge of the table. Covered dishes, two liter bottles of soda and a couple of opaque milk jugs without labels sat on brightly colored tablecloths, while nine other people sat or stood around the long groaning board.

No one seemed to pay attention to our two police cars parked side to side at the edge of the gravel.

"Is that Andy Hughes wearing the blue wool jacket and Crocodile Dundee hat?" I asked Vern Hobbs.

"Yep. One with the rifle gun at his side."

"Stan, you take the right side near Andy. Junior, Bobby, you guys in the middle. I'll speak to Big Jake. I assume he's the monster on the left."

"That's him, green plaid shirt and brown hat," Vern said.

"Harley, back up Stan. Vern, cover my end. Any questions?"

We had already rehearsed our act back at the PD, so there were none. Junior moved his car, and we advanced on the picnickers like the Earp brothers and Doc Holliday stalking the Clantons and McLaurys at the OK Corral.

People began noticing us when we stood a couple yards from the tables. The dancers stopped dancing and as soon as the musicians spotted me and the uniformed cops, they stopped playing. I thought it had gotten quiet enough to hear myself blink, but I was probably mistaken.

I made eye contact with my target. "Jake MacGregor? My name's Sam Jenkins from Prospect Police. We need to talk."

Before MacGregor could respond, I heard Stanley. "Don't move that hand, Mr. Hughes. Leave the rifle be. Good. Now, how about you put both hands flat on the table?"

Instinct would cause most people to look at what was happening, but for a cop, that could be a costly mistake. Stan and Harley Flatt knew how to control a situation. I kept my eyes on Jake MacGregor and wondered if Andy was packing the Colt handgun LeRoy McMurray mentioned.

"What's this about?" Jake asked.

"You know exactly what it's about," I said. "And I think you've been waiting to hear from us."

MacGregor nodded.

"First thing we're going to do is compare that 38-55 Winchester your cousin is carrying to the bullets that killed three men at Big Bear Creek and Wicher Kline. Bobby, confiscate that weapon."

A muffled buzz of voices passed through the crowd as Bobby Crockett fetched Andy's rifle and laid it on the ground when he resumed his position on Stanley's left.

A thin, dark-haired young man with a short scraggly beard and wearing Real-Tree camo clothing pushed his way up to the front of the crowd on my right, six or eight feet from Big Jake. He looked about as smart as a persimmon, so I assumed he was Roy MacGregor. Moments later, a shorter, little older young man, clean-shaven and with lighter brown hair took a spot close to Roy. Their camouflage jackets matched.

"I'd like you and your sons to come with us to the police station," I said. "I have a warrant to search your property for guns that might have been used at the campground, and the hide and meat from a bear those

North Carolina men killed."

Aside from a frown, Jake didn't show much emotion.

"County evidence technicians are standing by, ready to begin the search."

"Y'all ain't goin' inta my house," Jake said.

"Yeah, we are, Mr. MacGregor. But out of respect, I'll allow your wife to open up for those officers. That way, they don't have to kick in the door."

Jake ripped the fedora off his head and slapped it against his thigh. "Gat-dag it, Andy, Whatchew got ta say 'bout this?"

Andy began to stand when all 235 pounds of Stanley Rose pushed him down onto the bench seat.

With his hands back on the tabletop, Andy said, "Don't ya let nobody search yer house, Jake. You got the rot to a lawyer."

Jake looked at me.

"There is no doctor, lawyer or Indian chief in this county that's going to keep my men from executing that search warrant. Count on it. The paper's been signed by a judge."

Jake tossed his hat on the table and shook his head. "I never wanted me no trouble. Don't want no trouble now."

Andy stuck in his two cents again. "Ya got the rot ta remain silent, Jake. Shut the hell up!"

I looked toward Andy Hughes. "Cuff that man, Sarge, and lay him on the ground."

A buzz began traveling through the crowd again.

"Easy," I said. "Don't hurt him."

Big Jake sighed and looked ready to admit defeat. "What do I need ta do?"

I pointed at him and the two sons. "You three need to come with us. Your cousin is taken care of. Would you like to do this like gentlemen, or are we going to have a problem?"

"Told ya," Jake said, "don't want no trouble."

From the ground, Andy yelled, "Gotdamnit, Jake, if ya ain't under arrest, ya don't gotta go nowheres. You an' the boys stay put."

MacGregor said, "Shut up, Andy, and lemme think." Jake looked at his sons and then back at me.

"What's it going to be, Jake?"

He turned to his left. "L'il Will, 'Simmon Head, come here, boys."

Will moved, but Persimmon Head stood fast.

"Roy," a woman with long brown hair and a dark mole on her cheek said, "go to your daddy, son."

The boy still didn't move.

Will stood next to his father now and looked back at his brother. "Come on, "'Simmon Head, let's git this done."

Roy shook his head.

Andy yelled again. "That's it, boy. Stand yer ground. Stay where yer at."

Stanley placed a foot on Andy's neck and pushed down, stifling his last word.

Young Roy hung his head. His shoulders moved up and down a little, and his breathing appeared labored. Then he picked his head up, yelled, "Whooo-eee!" lifted his jacket with one hand and reached for the butt of a revolver with the other.

"Gun!" I yelled. I crouched, reached for my pistol and heard a shot fired.

My ears rang from the noise and concussion within the confined area. The shot echoed off the rock face behind the stream. Mrs. MacGregor and a few other women screamed and covered their eyes. She sank to her knees and reached for her son.

Junior Huskey rushed forward, grabbed a six inch Colt Trooper still tucked into the waistband of Roy MacGregor's pants and checked for a pulse.

Little Will joined his mother. Harlan Flatt moved up close to the edge of the tables and looked menacing with his black AR-15 at port arms. He visually scanned the crowd, but they all seemed to be fixated on the body of Roy MacGregor.

Immediately after the shot was fired, Carver and Finch pulled into the parking area, their truck skidding to a stop on the gravel. Stanley used his portable radio to call for an ambulance and any available county or state units for backup.

Junior looked at me, the fingers of his left hand placed across the boy's carotid artery, the big .357 revolver in his right hand. He shook his head. A blood stain was spreading across Roy's yellow shirt, visible through his half open jacket.

Bobby Crockett said, "Cancel that ambulance."

Stanley keyed the transmit button again. "Put a hold on the medics. Make that a crime scene unit and the ME."

The radio crackled. "Is everyone okay?" Bettye asked.

"One civilian down." Stan said. "No other injuries."

"10-4, unit five-three-five," she said.

I returned the Smith and Wesson to its holster and stepped close to Jake MacGregor. His body seemed frozen, but his face twitched as he fought back the tears that glazed his eyes.

"Why in hell did the boy do that?" I asked, and immediately realized he couldn't answer my question. But I was wrong.

Jake tilted his head and looked me in the eye. "Cause the damn fool wanted ta be like his Uncle Andy."

I snapped the safety on my holster and put a hand on Jake's shoulder. "I'm sorry for your loss."

I couldn't count the number of times I'd used those words, and they always seemed hollow and inadequate.

Jake nodded, picked up his hat and placed it on his head. "Bible says pride is wrong. This was all 'bout my pride and some gat-dag bear hide. I'm the one who's sorry."

I waved over the two TWRA officers and asked them to cuff Jake and Little Will.

I found Vern Hobbs standing where I last saw him, holding his bolt action rifle across his chest. He had bitten his toothpick in half.

"You okay?" I asked.

He shook his head, but didn't answer for a long moment. "I never did kill a human b'fore. Stupid—young—sombitch. Why'd he go fer his gun?"

I shrugged. "We'll never know."

"S'pose ya want this." He handed me the Remington 30-06.

I opened the bolt, pocketed the spent cartridge and pushed the safety on. "I don't know who the kid planned to shoot, but I'm guessing it was me. Thank you."

Vern nodded. "Yep." He turned, walked over to my car and sat in the back seat.

* * * *

"I didn't even have time to leave the room before the Grand Jury declared Vern's shooting justified," Moira Menzies said.

We were sitting in her corner office on the third floor of the Blount County Justice Center. She was wearing a wine-colored two piece suit with a knee length, straight skirt. She's a pretty woman and has good legs for a girl over fifty. The color complimented her blonde hair.

"Good," I said. "Does he know?"

"He waited around. I told him."

"Thanks."

"I like the way you wrote up the shooting incident. You ever work for Internal Affairs in New York?"

I shook my head. "Bite your tongue."

She smiled and chuckled silently.

"I'm sure you heard Bill Werner matched Andy Hughes's 38-55 to four of the bodies," I said. "Jake's .35 Marlin killed one, as did Roy's .357 Colt."

She nodded.

"Will's statement confirms that he used the shotgun we found in the loft over Jake's repair shop at Big Bear Creek. They didn't contest anything."

"Jake and Will MacGregor are both using Joe Costello as their lawyer. They asked to be tried together." Moira made a face and tossed the pen she'd been holding onto her desktop. "I wonder who suggested him?"

"Beats me. Joe has a good reputation."

"How do you suppose they can afford him?"

"Family plan? You'd have to ask Joe."

"Yeah, right."

"They taking a plea?"

"Asked for manslaughter one," she said.

"You agree to it?"

"If they do the max. Those were cold-blooded killings, but a plea would save time and money."

"Very cold," I said. "And fifteen years gives a man time to reflect on his prior bad behavior. I doubt you're looking at recidivists."

"You sound like a social worker."

I laughed. "How about Hughes?"

"No great deals, but his public defender says he'll plead guilty to murder for no death penalty."

"No parole, I hope."

"I want to see him die in jail." Moira spoke with a little venom in her voice.

"And let the rats eat his ears off," I said, remembering Vern Hobbs' earlier statement.

She looked at me like I had two heads. "Oh, yuck. That's gross."

THE END

Ode to Willie Joe

Wayne Zurl

Dedication

*To FRC and the 2,700,000 who also served,
and the 58,000 who didn't come home.
Don't call me captain any more.*

Ode to Willie Joe
Wayne Zurl

Willie Joe Ballantyne received a silver star and two purple hearts for his service in Vietnam. I knew this because around the 20th of each month, I'd see him take the medals to the Foothills Pawn Shop and get a few bucks to hold him until his VA disability check arrived. In addition to being a genuine war hero, Willie Joe was a raging alcoholic.

At 10:30 on a beautiful Friday night in June, Willie Joe landed in my soup. Half way through an episode of *Blue Bloods,* the phone rang. Sergeant Stan Rose spoke to me.

"Look, I'm sorry, boss, but he's insisting on seeing you personally."

"Why?" I asked. I'd been looking forward to going to bed at eleven o'clock and not spending quality time with someone arrested for public intoxication.

"I'm not sure. He's looped and talking about how you saved him in Vietnam, and then he goes off on… You're going to love this—how tonight he saw a UFO and a couple of green spacemen."

"Oh, for chrissakes."

"Please, bawana, I be owin' ya fo dis."

"You can't schmooze me with your Uncle Remus act."

"I can try."

"You people take advantage of me."

"Who?"

I sighed. "I'll be there in twenty minutes."

Kate had opened the windows earlier that evening. Dry, seventy degree, invigorating air wafted through the living room at less than five miles per hour. If I had to go back to work, I'd do it in style. And so, Kate helped me put the top down on my restored '67 Austin-Healey.

She kissed my cheek. "See you later, sweetie."

"I won't be long, but I'll probably need a drink after this."

She kissed me again, this time on the lips and a little longer. "My poor boy."

I dropped into the driver's seat, turned the key and touched the starter. The big Phase Two engine grumbled and I backed out of the garage.

Fifteen minutes later, I tapped my four digit code into the lock on the back door of Prospect PD. Stan Rose, all six-feet-four-inches and two-hundred and thirty-five pounds of him, sat in front of a computer in the squad room, completing the arrest package on Willie Joe Ballantyne.

"Where's our guest?" I asked.

He handed me a ring with two large brass keys attached.

As soon as I opened the outer door to the cell block, a combination of body odor and the sour smell of a fully matriculated drunk assaulted me. I opened the inner bars and cranked open four casement windows across from the D cells.

After making enough noise to wake our only visitor, I watched him rub his eyes and struggle to get off the wooden slab we call a prisoner's bed.

Unshaven and disheveled, sixty-four year old Willie Joe stood, swayed for a long moment, steadied himself and took a few steps to grab the bars that separated us.

"What's the haps, Willie?"

"Oh, Captain, thank God ya here."

His breath rocked me. I took an involuntary step backward.

"I'm not in the Army any more, Willie Joe."

"Yeah, but I cain't fergit how yew and yer men saved our bacon. I owe ya fer that—ferever."

"Forget it, partner. We were just doing our job. Now, what's the problem tonight?"

"Spacemen."

"Huh?"

"Yessir, spacemen. I seen two o' them, a'glowin' green. I seen 'em."

Ode to Willie Joe

When I took the job as chief of police in Prospect, the local papers and TV stations told all of East Tennessee about the retired New York detective moving to the Smokies and taking over at a department recently scarred by scandal. A day later, Willie Joe walked into my office saying he recognized my name as the officer in charge of the Mike Force who reinforced his infantry platoon and drove away over two-hundred Viet Cong surrounding them. All that happened in 1969. Over the years, Willie's brain may have gotten pickled, but his memory never faded.

"Where'd you see these little green men?"

"In the woods jest north o' Crystal Creek an' half a klick east o' Prospect Road."

"Place they call Campbell's Woods, right?"

"Yessir."

"What were you doing there after dark?"

"Takin' a shortcut home."

Willie Joe lived in an ancient single-wide behind a truck repair shop off Sevierville Road, just a long walk from the center of town.

"Tell me what you saw."

"Two o' them was workin' in the woods."

"Doing what?"

"Don't know. They was short—real short, close ta the ground, doin' somethin'. I didn't git too close 'cause I figgered they's armed.

"They had weapons?"

"I jest figgered. Wouldn't you be?"

I couldn't remember the last time I invaded another planet.

"You saw a space ship?" I asked.

"I looked fer one."

"Did you see it?"

"Mebbe."

Getting other than raw, unconfirmed intelligence from my soldier friend seemed improbable.

"How much did you drink tonight?" I asked.

"A big bottle o' wine."

"Big bottle? A half-gallon?"

"I guess."

"Maybe more?"

"I kinda lost track."

Why was I not surprised?

"Some drinkers tell me they've seen pink elephants."

"I weren't seein' things, Captain, I swear." He clutched the bars tighter, pressed his face against the bars and looked even more pathetic. "They's little green men—least I thought they's men. Mighta been women."

I tried to dodge his breath again and felt the beginning of a tension headache.

"What happened after you saw the green people?"

"Ran back ta town. Hardees' was the first place I found. I tried ta git he'p, but nobody believed me."

"And someone called the police."

"Yessir."

"Because you got a little rambunctious in the burger joint."

He pushed the straggly gray hair out of his eyes and looked sheepish.

"Guess so."

Every time I see Willie Joe, I feel sorry for him and all the guys in the same boat.

"You been eating regularly?"

"I git by."

"Got money for the rest of the month?"

"Some."

"The judge should give you from three to five days. At least you'll have three hots and a cot for that long. You can dry out, too."

"I guess. But last time, when that trooper arrested me, I didn't like the crowd in county. They's been letting in too many derelicts."

I rolled my eyes. "Take care of yourself, Willie Joe."

I turned to leave, but before I could lock the inner bars, he called out.

"Promise me, Captain, ya'll check that spot in the woods. Won't take ya long—jest a little recon. Ya need ta save this town, an' I know ya kin do it."

I just love public confidence.

136

"I'll look into it, partner. Get some sleep."

After I closed the cell block door, I tried to suck all the fresh air from the hallway into my lungs. Back in the squad room, I handed the keys to Stanley.

"Situation resolved?" he asked.

"Yeah, I'll take my ray gun and decoder ring into the woods and do battle with the spacemen."

He laughed and hit the print button on the computer. Willie Joe's arrest paperwork began to emerge from the printer.

"I'm a hopeless schlep, Stanley." I peeled off a twenty from the bills I carried in the front pocket of my jeans. "Put this in the envelope with his property."

"Got any free samples for me?"

"You owe me for interrupting my night."

"Dat's why y'all git da big bucks, Bwana."

* * * *

Before going to work on Monday, I stopped at the Foothills Pawn Shop. The owner, a Cherokee man named Lucius Timberlake, sat on a stool behind the counter, a cup of coffee and open newspaper in front of him. Luscious was my age, had a full head of long dark hair which he wore parted in the center and pulled back into a ponytail. He'd retired from the Army after thirty years and became one of the most honest pawn brokers I'd ever met. Lucius looked like he posed for the obverse of the buffalo nickel.

"Morning, Lucius."

He answered in Cherokee. "Si yu, Chief."

"Isn't that what I'm supposed to call you?"

"You are dating yourself, white eyes."

"We sound like actors in an old western movie."

"Want me to tell you about when I was a scout for the long knives?" He spoke seriously, but his almost black eyes were full of mischief.

"I want you to tell me about Willie Joe Ballantyne. He been acting especially strange lately."

"He pawned his medals again last week. He did not seem any different than usual."

Lucius spoke with an accent particular to many Native Americans.

"How much do you give him each month?"

"Fifty dollars."

"Are you being kind to another veteran, or is his stuff worth that much?"

"I am not sure too many pawn dealers would give him fifty dollars, but if he never picked them up again, I could sell the grouping for perhaps five-hundred, maybe more."

"No kidding?"

"I made him give me a copy of his DD-214. Those separation papers say he is entitled to everything he owns—a named Silver Star, pair of Purple Hearts and Good Conduct Medal. Plus all the campaign medals and a couple of sterling badges. That would be a good catch for a collector. He may abuse the fire water, but those medals are important to him. He is a straight shooter and always comes back."

"He was hitting the fire water the other night and created a scene at Hardees. Said he saw a couple of little green spacemen."

Lucius took a sip of coffee to hide a smile. "Where?"

"Campbell's Woods."

"Hmmm."

"You've been here longer than me. Any other people report seeing strange things in those woods?"

"My people tell stories of many strange things the white man would fear. I will have to check my index of legends for little green men."

"You're a big help."

"That's what Custer said to his scout.

It rained very early the next morning, and by the time I arrived at work, the humidity had blown away, and I walked from my car to the municipal building in clear, crisp mountain air.

At 10:30 my intercom buzzed. Bettye Lambert, the loveliest desk sergeant on the planet decided to ruin my day.

"Sam, I've got a Mr. Grubbs here who wants to speak with you."

"Can't you help him? I'm up to my rump in this statistical garbage the mayor wants."

"This one's outta my league, boss. I'll show him in."

Sometimes I wonder who the police chief really is.

Bettye stepped into my office smiling. A small man, no less than eighty years old, stood next to her. He looked frail and upset. I tossed my glasses onto the desktop and stood. It's difficult to get mad at a beautiful blonde and a pathetic old man.

"Chief, this is Obed Grubbs," she said. "Mr. Grubbs, Chief Sam Jenkins."

"Sit down, sir." I pointed to one of the guest chairs in front of my desk. The old boy took a seat, and Bettye wiggled her fingers, waving good-bye.

"Sergeant Lambert says you have a problem. How can I help?"

"You'll probably think I'm crazy."

I tilted my head and frowned, wondering what would come next. "Try me."

"Didn't wanna say nothin' 'bout this, but Velma told me I better."

"Velma is your wife?"

"Yessir."

I offered an encouraging smile. "Well, Velma has spoken. It's too late to turn back."

He shrugged. "I'd appreciate it, sir, if ya didn't laugh.

"Go ahead, Mr. Grubbs, I'm quite the professional."

"Well, sir, I's takin' Rufus fer a walk last night 'bout ten o'clock, a'fore goin' ta bed—along that path through Campbell's Woods. Know where it is?"

I nodded and almost recited Willie Joe Ballantyne's description of the same location. "North of Crystal Creek and about a quarter mile east of Prospect Road."

"Zactly," he said. "I git ta the path from that end o' Blackberry Drive."

"What happened there?" I was afraid to hear his answer.

"Lord have mercy." He paused, shook his head and gently ran a hand over thinning white hair. "I seen a flyin' saucer."

I mustered up the energy and forced myself not to close my eyes and shake *my* head.

"Describe what you saw."

"Well, it was low ta the ground, jest a'hoverin' there."

"How close did you get?"

"Not sure. Soon as I seen it, I stopped as quick as a dawg who treed a coon.

"How big was it?"

"Not too big, but it was glowin' and green."

"Big as a car? Big as an elephant?"

"Not sure. Big enough ta carry them little men."

Things were going from bad to worse.

"You saw men?"

"Nosir, didn't say that. But I remember seein' pitchers o' spacemen on TV."

Normally, in police work, I'd say, 'Don't believe in coincidences.' But this was ridiculous.

"This thing was saucer shaped? Not like a rocket ship or anything?"

"Like I said, I didn't git too close. Looked sorta oval-like—and glowin' green."

Green spacemen and now green flying saucers. *Why me?*

"Can you show me the spot?" I asked.

"Me an' Rufus done run outta there pertty quick, but I guess so."

Bettye walked past my door carrying several case folders. Her hazel eyes twinkled over the tops of her granny glasses, and she showed me another big smile. I wanted to smack her.

"I'll follow you, Mr. Grubbs."

* * * *

An hour later, I walked back into the lobby of the PD and scowled at Bettye.

"Stanley got me Friday night, and now you get me today. Are you two in cahoots?"

"Darlin', nobody says cahoots anymore."

"Nobody sees flying saucers either. Willie Joe Ballantyne was drunk, and Mr. Grubbs wasn't wearing his glasses. I couldn't find a damn thing."

"Probably just a coincidence."

"I hate when you say that."

"What's the alternative?"

"Have you ever seen any green spacemen?"

She took a moment to chuckle. "I don't drink as much as you."

"That's a good idea. I'm going to Howell's for lunch, and I'm having a beer."

"Enjoy it, sugar. See you later."

* * * *

Tuesday morning, Kate turned on the little TV under the kitchen cabinets while we ate breakfast. The Today Show took a break, and local news from WNXX in Knoxville came on.

Between me chewing spoons full of bran flakes, the newscaster, a short blonde who wore a lot of eye makeup, shocked me.

"Yesterday," she said, "Obed Grubbs, of Prospect in Blount County, reported seeing a UFO on Sunday night. Reporter Rocky Bryte spoke with Mr. Grubbs."

They cut away from the studio and showed a young guy with dark, slicked down hair speaking to Obed Grubbs in front of the Grubbs' homestead. Rockwood Bryte stuck a microphone under the old man's chin, and I listened to a recount of his flying saucer story.

"Grrr," I said.

"You growled," Kate said.

"That old coot called the TV station."

Kate smiled over the top of her coffee cup. "You didn't tell me about the flying saucers."

"The old man came in yesterday. Wasn't worth mentioning."

Her big brown eyes narrowed, and she tried to hide a smile. "Two sightings in a couple of days. Must be true."

"Gimme a break."

She laughed and took another sip of coffee.

"The press loves this kind of crap," I said. "I'll have a dozen reporters crawling all over the office today, and every UFO hunter in the southeast is probably gassing up their cars as we speak. I am not a happy policeman."

* * * *

When I got to work at nine, I found Rocky the reporter sitting next to Bettye's desk, reading our computerized police blotter.

Bettye said, "Mornin', boss," and grimaced as I scowled at the reporter.

He stood. "Chief Jenkins, what have you learned about the UFOs that were reported in Prospect?"

"UFOs?" I planned on strangling Stanley for mentioning extraterrestrials in Willie Joe Ballantyne's arrest report—which was public record and available for the likes of Rockwood Bryte to read.

"The one Friday night and then again on Sunday."

I felt steam preparing to escape from my ears. "Grrr." I growled again.

"I beg your pardon?"

I took a deep breath. "I'll speak with you in a minute, Mr. Bryte, but I've got something important to do first."

I closed my office door, grabbed the phone and dialed Rachel Williamson's number. After five rings, the answering machine kicked in. I waited for the beep.

"I know you're there, and I know you only left work at midnight. I'm sorry to call this early, but wake up. Pick up the damn phone. Do something before I have a stroke."

Rachel is the evening news anchor on WNXX and my friend. Finally, the receiver clicked.

"Hi, what's wrong?" She sounded sleepy.

"I guess I woke you—sorry. Got a minute?"

"I'm listening."

"Is your husband home?"

"He's working."

"Kids there?"

"It's summer, of course."

"I need to talk."

"Obviously."

"How could you people do this to me?"

"Who people and what?"

"You NXX people. Young Rocky Bryte is sitting in my lobby waiting to talk to me about UFOs. Tell me you're not responsible for this."

I heard a faint snicker. "Of course I'm not. But I'm not the only news person at the station."

"I might kill Rocky and drop him in the woods for the little green men to take away."

"Don't be stupid."

"Then phone your station manager and tell him to call off Rockwood Bryte, boy reporter."

"Don't get excited, Sammy, I'll fix this."

I let out a puff of air. "Good. Thank you."

"Talk to the man for a few minutes. That should satisfy him. After I call George, Rocky won't bother you anymore. Okay?"

"Grrr!"

"You growled at me."

"I need a drink."

"Oh, stop. It's only ten after nine. You don't need one. You just want it."

"Same thing."

"I'll talk to you later. Be nice to Rocky."

"Grrr."

"You're so sweet. Bye."

Rachel hung up. I walked out to the lobby. Knoxville's version of Jimmy Olsen jumped up. If he had a microphone, I believe he would have stuck it in my face.

"You wanted to see me?" I asked, trying to smile.

"Chief Jenkins, what have you done to shed some light on these UFO sightings?"

I took another deep breath and reactivated my press conference smile.

"Come inside...Rocky. Let's talk."

I made an about-face and headed to my office, wanting to step on the little creep's neck.

The cub reporter sat on the edge of my guest chair, notebook in hand. I slumped into my big swivel chair and waited.

"Have you sent search parties to check the Campbell's Woods area?" he asked. His voice dripped with anticipation. He must have been taking the whole thing seriously, the nitwit.

"Search parties?" I felt another tension headache about to crash into my forehead.

"You are going to see if something happened, aren't you?"

Instead of throwing my stapler at him, I took a moment and answered civilly. "I checked the area myself and found nothing."

"Why would two people claim to see extraterrestrials and spacecraft in the same area only days apart?"

The mayor would owe me a commendation after this was over. Not for having any special talent and solving an inter-galactic mystery, but for having the restraint necessary not to strangle certain people. After a short pause, I answered.

"One was falling down drunk, and the other is quite old and wasn't wearing his glasses."

Rocky waited for a long moment to comment. I used every ounce of restraint I had not to scream at the young imbecile.

"Oh," he said. "Well, will you...?"

I interrupted. "I plan on assigning two men to search the area tonight at approximately the same time as these two not-so-reliable witnesses thought they saw something unusual."

"Oh." He pulled a business card out of his top pocket and dropped it on my desk. "Will you call me with the results?"

"I'd love to."

"Uh, thanks."

"Don't mention it."

He just sat there.

"Do we have any other business?" I asked.

"Uh, no. Thanks for your time."

"You betcha."

He stood and offered me a hand. I shook it, but didn't pull him forward and tweak his nose. After a few seconds, Rockwood Bryte turned and walked out.

* * * *

At 3:30 Stan Rose walked in, prepared to supervise the four-to-twelve shift.

"Hey, boss man, what's the haps?"

"The haps, young sergeant, is I have an assignment for you and one of your minions."

"Minions?"

"Myrmidons, if you like."

"I don't be likin' da sound o' dat, sahib."

"Who's working the cars tonight?"

"Junior and Bobby John."

"Good. Use Junior. He wants to be a detective. This may squelch his ambition. Search Campbell's Woods around ten o'clock and see what you can find."

"Like moon men?"

"Sure. Moon men, Martians, space ships. I'm easy. If you find something, call me."

"As you wish, great white leader."

* * * *

At 11:15 that night, the phone rang. I had just gotten out of the shower and wanted to read a couple chapters in my latest James Lee Burke novel. Instead, Stan Rose gave me some news.

"I don't want to get on your shit list for calling late," he said, "but you'll want to see this."

"I want to go to bed, Stanley. What's so important?"

"We searched the area like you asked."

"And?"

"And we found the glowing green stuff."

"Green stuff?"

"Junior the woodsman calls it foxfire."

"I've heard of foxfire, some kind of luminescent fungus that clings to decaying wood. So what? A drunk and a myopic old coot might think it was a flying saucer. We can write the whole thing off. Why call me now?"

"We also found a spot where someone did some digging—trying to hide something."

"You find anything?"

"Yeah, a body. A very small one."

* * * *

Campbell's Woods covered about fifty acres between a residential development and the farm fields stretching toward the border of neighboring Seymour. I parked in the cul-de-sac of Blackberry Drive and, using a flashlight to illuminate my way, walked over a well-worn path under tall tulip poplars, sweet gums and Virginia pines.

I don't know how far I walked, but when I reached a moderate-sized clearing, I thought I had just stepped into a night baseball game. Jackie Shuman and David Sparks, crime scene investigators from the county sheriff's office, had set up enough portable lighting to give a blind man vision.

Those two puttered around doing what forensic investigators do while Doctor Morris Rappaport, the deputy medical examiner, and his assistant Earl Ogle worked over a very small, colorless corpse.

I stood over the pathologist for only a moment before he looked up.

"Hell of a thing, Sam."

"Got any first impressions?"

"Hard to say just now. This isn't something we encounter every day."

"Understood."

"After the post I'll know better what we've got here."

"Yeah, but just off the top of your head, what do you figure?"

"I'd say, twenty-three, twenty-four weeks."

I shook my head. "Jeez. Abortion?"

"Maybe. Maybe miscarriage. I'll know more *after* the autopsy."

A small, shallow grave ten feet from the doctor had been excavated and outlined with stakes and yellow crime scene tape.

"I'm going to speak with Jackie. How long are you going to be?"

"Not long," Mo said.

I faced the two deputies and called to the senior man, "Jackie, can we have a word?"

Thirty-five-year-old Jackie Shuman had been a cop for fourteen years. He was one of the most thorough evidence technicians I've known.

"Doin' aw right t'day, Sam?"

"Just peachy, kid. You and David dig up the body?"

"Did most o' the work. Stanley and Junior called us. They found the spot where the ground had been disturbed. They did a little lookin' and found the fetus, but didn't want to disturb things."

"Animals get to it?"

"No. Somethin' tried ta dig it up, but didn't make much progress. "'Possum, maybe. I figure a coon woulda kept diggin'. They's tenacious boogers."

"I'll talk to my guys soon, but what made them look here?"

"Foxfire."

"Stan mentioned that. I know what it is, but I've never seen it."

"If ya walked up here without all these lights, you'd see it glowin' green. Some o' the old mountain folks call it fairy fire. Couple clumps are attached to that dead log yonder, next ta the grave."

I looked where he pointed and saw a pair of fungus clumps, one almost eighteen inches across and the other slightly smaller.

"Big enough for a drunk and an old guy who can't see well to think they're little space ships."

"Do what?" He looked at me like I had two heads.

"Don't ask, Jackie."

He took off his ball cap and scratched his short dark hair. "You got it, boss."

"Gonna finish the paperwork tonight?" I asked.

"At time and a half, you bet."

"Give it to one of my midnight shift guys. I'll look at it in the morning."

"You got that, too."

* * * *

The next morning, I collapsed into the chair next to Bettye's desk just as the radio crackled.

"Five-oh-nine, headquarters. Got me a ten-ten, fender-bender in the parkin' lot behind the stores, east side o' the town square. No injury and no wrecker needed." PO Billy Puckett sounded a little scratchy.

"Ten-four, five-zero-nine," Bettye said, and time stamped a central complaint card. "CC for paperwork is 11-2,462."

Puckett acknowledged her transmission, and she turned to me.

"Mornin', darlin'. My, but don't you look tired."

"I got home at three this morning and wasn't in the mood to sleep."

"I've read over the crime scene reports Jackie Shuman dropped off. I guess this explains our little green space ships."

"After Mo and Earl removed the fetus, Jackie turned off the lights so I could see the foxfire glow."

"Pretty, isn't it?"

"Shines like the northern lights."

"What did Dr. Mo say about the body?"

"Maybe twenty-four weeks."

"That old? If it was aborted, that's a crime."

"Yeah, but how am I going to find the female who carried the baby if there's no DNA on file?"

"Won't be easy." Bettye pushed her reading glasses out of the way and put her elbows on the desktop. "This kind of thing happens too often. Sometimes I wonder if these people think incest is a regional sport."

"That's one possibility."

"Makes me so mad."

"Could just be someone who's never heard of birth control. Kids today think *hooking up* is no different than playing handball."

"That makes me mad, too."

"I hear you. And how many women of child bearing age live in the area?"

Bettye shrugged.

"Hell of a suspect pool," I said.

She nodded.

Rhetorically, I asked, "Where do I start?"

She had an idea. "The nurse at Heritage High School might be a help."

"School officials never want to cooperate."

"Try her. She seems like a good person."

"School girls do get pregnant. Probably a good place to start."

"Could be."

"Know her?" I asked.

"We've met."

"Maybe you should do this."

She smiled. "I'll do anything you ask, Sammy."

I raised my eyebrows twice and tried to look lecherous. "Lord have mercy!"

* * * *

After a stop at home to change into civilian clothes, Bettye drove to the high school in nearby Maryville. At eleven o'clock, she walked back into the office wearing a simple, dark green sleeveless dress and conservative heels. I spun the desk sergeant's chair around to face her.

"Solve the case, *Detective* Sergeant Lambert?"

She sat in a chair next to the big desk.

"Do I get something extra for workin' out of job title?"

"My undying gratitude."

"Yew are jest the sweetest man." She gave her southern accent a little more country twang.

"And I'm devilishly cute."

"I agree with that and remember I said so when I tell you I didn't learn a blessed thing."

I shook my head. "Must be an older woman."

"Maybe, but we can't be sure."

"The people in school would have noticed a girl six months pregnant walking around."

"Not necessarily. If the fetus wasn't well developed and she wore loose clothing to hide it, she may only have looked like she put on a little weight."

"How about the parents?"

"I hate to say this, but sometimes mothers don't pay attention to their children."

"So we're back to square one."

"Sorry."

I began to feel sorry for myself and thought if I'd ever been a parent, I'd damn sure notice if my daughter had gotten pregnant. Then the radio squawked. Billy Puckett was calling again.

"Five-oh-nine, headquarters, I'm goin' ten-thirty-two with one female for criminal mischief at the mini-mall on McTeer's Station Pike. Mileage is 66,192."

I keyed the mike. "Ten-four, five-oh-nine. Time is 11:08. Advise when ten-three-six."

* * * *

Officer Billy Puckett escorted Dorie Huffaker into the lobby six minutes later. Bettye booked in the prisoner, and I asked about the arrest.

"I couldn't believe it," Puckett said. "I's sittin' right there, big as life, in the parkin' lot, doin' paperwork and this one," he jerked a thumb at the sulking young redhead in handcuffs, "keys a brand new Chevy."

"Much damage?"

"Oh, yeah. Front and rear fenders and both doors."

"Yikes. Call Ralph Fleenor's Body Shop for an estimate. This is probably a felony. You're having a busy day."

"Tell me about it."

I turned to the prisoner, a pretty but somewhat hard-looking girl. "What do you do for a living, Ms. Huffaker?"

She lifted her head and took a long moment to answer. "I couldn't find work this summer. I start my senior year at Heritage in August."

"You're seventeen?"

"Yes."

She looked twenty-five.

"Been arrested before?"

"Picked up for pot once."

"What happened in court?"

"Plead guilty so they'd make it a violation and not a misdemeanor."

"Caught with a little weight?

"Like an ounce."

"You're old enough to charge as an adult now, and the judge may not give you youthful offender status with a prior conviction. You've got yourself a jackpot, young lady."

She hung her head again.

"Officer Puckett will advise you of your rights, but since he caught you in the act, we don't have to ask you squat. Although you've got the right to remain silent, I've got the right to tell you how the system works." But she didn't give me an opportunity to speak further.

"I only did it because that Ashley Teeter is such a bitch. She's, like, always actin' like she's better than other people, always hassling me, and…"

I held up a hand to stop her.

"That's what's called a spontaneous admission. Don't say any more until the officer tells you that you can call a lawyer. And we'll even let you call your parents."

"Y'all, like, have ta tell my parents?"

"If damage to the car is over fifteen-hundred dollars—and it's probably double that, you'll be charged with felony criminal mischief. You'll be taken for arraignment and probably offered bail. That might be five-hundred dollars or five-thousand. It's up to the judge. Got that much cash in your purse?"

"Five-thousand dollars?"

"Who knows?"

"Oh, man."

"You may need mom and dad to pay the freight. A bail bondsman will loan the money to your parents, but not you. They'll get an opportunity to put up collateral and get the bail posted if they don't have that much cash handy"

She shook her head and for the first time, seemed to realize how much trouble she was in. "We're, like, not rich."

"Or you can sit in the county lockup until your trial."

Both Billy and Bettye knew where I was heading. Puckett grinned, and Bettye let a slight smile cross her lips.

Dorie Huffaker closed her eyes and continued to shake her head.

"I think, Dorie, you need a friend at Prospect PD."

"Do what?"

"Let me explain how the world goes around."

We adjourned to the squad room where Billy cuffed her to a three-inch steel ring attached to a desk. I asked if she wanted a soda.

"Mountain Dew. Ya want me ta pay?"

"This one's on the house."

I returned two minutes later.

"Okay, here's the bottom line." I took a side chair and spun it around, sitting with my elbows resting on the back. "We're going to charge you with a crime that carries a maximum sentence of seven years."

Dorie's green eyes bulged.

"If you want to ride that out on your own, fine. If your lawyer asks for a plea bargain, I'll say no. Officer Puckett caught you in the act—no big deal to us. No hard feelings either. You do the jail time, and we get paid every other Thursday."

She swallowed hard. "Jail time?"

I shrugged. "Yeah. You'll probably only do one third of the seven years if you behave yourself inside. So, let me see…" I made a production out of figuring the actual time. "That makes two years and four months."

"Two years in jail? For, like, keyin' a car? Are you crazy?"

I smiled. "Don't forget the four months. And I'm not crazy. You damaged a brand new Chevy Cruze—nice little car by the way. The law is like a scale. The more money that's involved, the more time you do. Things even out. Understand?"

"I can't believe this."

"Did Ashley's parents buy her the new car?"

"I guess."

"Judges are elected officials, and the Teeters can vote. Easy way to get two more votes is put away the person who screwed up the new car they bought."

"I cannot believe this."

"You said that before. Let's get back to how the system works. It's simple. You need a favor. But we don't do favors on account."

She looked confused.

"You'd have to do something for us first."

Now she looked frightened. Billy Puckett clicked around on the computer, bringing up the arrest report form to fill out. I elaborated for Dorie.

"You'd have to give us information that leads to an arrest of someone badder than you."

"You, like, want me to rat out one o' my friends?"

"Smart girl."

"Oh, man!"

"Look, it's up to you. You can buy yourself a three-hundred dollar an hour attorney, pay your bail, and tough it out. Or you can buy yourself a friend here with information that's quite free. If I like what I hear, I'll ask the assistant district attorney to let the judge release you without bail, and when you plead guilty to misdemeanor criminal mischief, I'll recommend probation and community service."

"No jail?"

"No jail, no bail, no hassle."

"Honest?"

"Trust me. I know what I'm doing."

She chewed her bottom lip and thought for a moment.

"Ya mean, like, I'd have ta pick up trash on the highway?"

"Something like that."

"And report to a probation officer?"

"Maybe once a week to start. Then once a month for a total of three years would be my guess."

She thought some more.

"And no jail?"

"Yep."

"What do y'all want ta know?"

* * * *

I rearranged assignments to accommodate questioning Dorie Huffaker. Billy Puckett worked in the squad room processing the arrest package. PO Joey Gillespie came in to work the desk, and Bettye joined me and Dorie in my office. Bettye's presence would protect me if Dorie's lawyer decided to have her claim I made inappropriate requests of her. We all sat in the guest chairs in front of my desk.

"Okay," I said, "what do you know that can buy your freedom?"

She looked pleased with herself. "You can buy pot, and lots of it, off o'..."

Before she could finish, I spoke a little more forcefully than necessary. "Dorie, stop! Do I look like I care about pot?"

Her eyes widened and she looked disappointed. "Like, I don't know. You're a cop, right? And selling pot is, like, a crime."

"I want to hear something good, not about some moron selling marijuana. Tell me something more serious than felony criminal mischief."

"Like, how do I know what that is?"

Bettye, the good cop, added her thoughts. "Think of something you wouldn't want to get caught doin'. Don't hold back, Dorie. Your future is on the line here."

"I, like, don't know people who rob banks or anything."

"But," I said, "It's hard to go through life not knowing someone who's committed a serious crime. Burglarized a house, stolen a car and never ditched it, committed an unsolved sex crime."

She picked up her head and raised her eyebrows.

"You're a smart girl," I said. "You get the idea."

Dorie thought for a long moment. "Maybe I can still get even with little Miss Ashley Teeter." She broke a smile. "Is it a crime to get an abortion? I mean, like murder?"

Sometimes I think I'm the greatest detective in the world. *Can I exploit a situation or what?*

I did my best not to smile when I said, "It depends on several things. First is how far along the pregnancy has gone."

"Like, long."

"Explain what you know, Dorie," Bettye said.

"Y'all're, like, not gonna tell anyone I told ya about this, are ya?"

Bettye answered. "No. We only have to tell the ADA and the judge. Everything you say is confidential."

I was beginning to get impatient. "Just tell us what you know, and we'll decide if it's a crime"

I wasn't sure if Dorie trusted us, but she continued.

"Well," she said, "I know for a fact that Ashley got pregnant during school. She started missing periods in, like, March, maybe. So, what's that, at about three months?"

"Could be," Bettye said.

"Now it's, like, end o' June. That's six or seven months, and now she's not pregnant anymore."

"Did Ashley tell you she had an abortion?" I asked.

"I just saw her—no more baby."

"Did she go to someone? Do it herself? What?"

"I, like, don't know, but I hear she did it herself, and they got rid of it."

"They?"

"Her and Troy."

"He's the father?

"Far as I know, she's only hooked up with one guy. Troy Suttles."

"They both live in Prospect?"

"Uh-huh."

* * * *

Ashley Teeter was petite with short dark hair, a pale complexion and the look of a little rich girl. Bettye took her into the juvenile interview room and closed the door. A few minutes later, PO Bobby Crockett brought in Troy Suttles. I met them in the squad room and handed Troy a cola.

"Am I under arrest?" the kid asked.

He was also short, dark and might not have weighed a hundred-and-thirty soaking wet—the second member of our pair of little space persons. From the look of his clothing, his old man wasn't hurting for bucks either.

"No," I said, "we're just going to have a chat."

"'Bout what?"

"I'll be with you in a minute."

I walked across the hall and entered the juvie room without knocking.

"Hi, Ashley, I'm Chief Jenkins." I handed her a second can of soda. "I'll be back after you and Sergeant Lambert have a chance to talk."

"Okay," she said and picked up the can of soda.

I smiled like a Dutch uncle and left.

Back in the squad room, I laid an open penal law book on the desk in front of Troy Suttles. I stepped behind him and read a short passage while looking over his shoulder.

"A person is guilty of abortion in the first degree if he causes or assists in causing the termination of a fetus more than twenty-four weeks old. Abortion in the first degree is a class C felony." I slapped the book closed. "You don't know what a class C felony is so, you'd have to look in the front of the book to find out. But I'll save you the trouble. A class C felony can put you away for up to fifteen years. Add to that, a charge of unlawfully disposing of a body and someone—like you—could spend a long time in state prison."

Troy Suttles was about to take another sip of soda, but unsteadily placed the can back on the desk, straightened up and glared at me defiantly. But his face betrayed him. He was frightened, and the attempt to act cool became meaningless.

"Why are ya tellin' me this, sir?"

I opted for the silent treatment and just stared into his eyes. He didn't last thirty seconds.

"I didn't he'p with no abortion."

I waited few more seconds, sniffed, and said, "Says you." Then more silence.

Twenty seconds later, he said, "I don't know what you're talkin' about."

"Yes, you do."

After another twenty seconds, "Are you arrestin' me?"

"Not yet."

"Then I wanna go."

I picked up his soda can.

"Sure, you can leave—now that I've got your DNA on the soda can."

Bobby Crocket stood there grinning like a Cheshire cat. He folded his arms across his chest and looked like he was enjoying himself.

"The lab will analyze this and match you as the father of the fetus we found in the woods. And the next time I see you, it'll be in cuffs." I stood and put my face only inches from his right ear. "And then, I won't be in the mood to offer you a deal for cooperation."

"Do what?"

"Bobby, give me five minutes and then drive him anywhere he wants to go."

I walked out and reentered the juvenile room.

I smiled at Bettye. "Sarge, does Ashley know why she's here?"

"She does," Bettye said.

"Have anything to say?"

"Not yet."

"Okay." I picked up her soda can. "Pepsi from Troy and Dr. Pepper from you. I'll send them to the lab for a DNA test and match them with that poor little fetus we found in Campbell's Woods."

"You can't do that." Ashley tried her best to sound indignant. "That's illegal search and seizure...or something."

"Sure I can, and no, it's not. You guys are seventeen, and I plan on treating you as adults."

She folded her arms across her chest defensively and slouched a little in the chair.

"Oh, by the way," I said. "Troy the hero wants to leave. He's putting this all on you. Says he had nothing to do with anything."

"What?" Her face completely changed, and she sounded shocked.

"Quite the stand-up guy, isn't he?"

Ashley couldn't have looked sadder if I said her dog was squashed by a steam roller.

"In a couple of minutes," I said, "look out the window and watch the police officer drive Troy home."

Ashley wrinkled her brow and began to look truly concerned about her future.

"What did he tell you?" she asked cautiously.

"I guess he thinks you really can have an immaculate conception."

The small girl sat forward and rested her elbows on the table. Her face showed abject defeat, and she looked about twelve years old. "He said that?"

"Your pregnancy, your problem. Is he a nice guy or what?"

"My problem?" Her voice cracked. "That's not what he told me."

Bettye spoke softly. "What did Troy tell you, Ashley?"

Ashley slapped her palms on the desktop. "He's the only guy I ever slept with." Tears rolled down her left cheek. "He said he'd stick by me and do the right thing."

I softened my tone. "Tell us about the abortion, Ashley." I wondered when she would ask to call her parents.

"He called it an abortion?"

I raised my eyebrows and shrugged, but said nothing.

"There was no abortion. I miscarried." She wiped her nose with the back of her hand, sat back, and slouched again. "That lying bastard."

Ashley kept talking. I walked outside and told Bobby Crockett not to take Troy anywhere.

* * * *

Bettye and I took statements from Ashley and Troy. Neither ever asked to call a lawyer or their parents. At seventeen, they were adults in the eyes of the law and could make their own decisions.

After a few days, Doctor Rappaport confirmed that the young couple was, in fact, parents of the fetus, and after having Ashley examined, all the evidence pointed to an unfortunate but natural miscarriage.

I never pursued charges of unlawful disposition of a body. Both Ashley and Troy cooperated, and I figured, sometimes teenagers make terrible decisions, and sometimes Mother Nature hands down enough punishment to fit any crime.

Several days later, Bettye buzzed my phone.

"You have a visitor."

"Who is it?"

"I'll send him in."

I hate when she does that.

Willie Joe Ballantyne gingerly stepped into my doorway and knocked on the jamb.

"I come in, Captain?"

I stood up and decided not to press the issue of him calling me captain. We shook hands. "Sure, have a seat."

He had shaved, washed his long hair, and stood there wearing a faded but clean, old jungle jacket with a 199th Infantry Brigade patch on his right shoulder and a combat infantryman's badge sewn over the left breast pocket.

"Naw," he said, "I cain't stay. Jest wanted ta thank ya. The judge gave me five days and ordered me ta AA meetin's. Gotta do eighty-eight in ninety days. And if I miss those two, I got ta have a damn good reason."

"Have a way to get to the meetings?"

"They's up in Rockford. Got me a bicycle. No big thing. Been to a few already."

I nodded. "You feeling okay?"

"Yessir, doin' fine. Ain't had a drink since I seen ya last."

I smiled, genuinely glad that he might be on the right track. "Good for you."

"Been sleepin' better since I stopped drinkin'."

I nodded. "Willie Joe, I didn't find any space men in Campbell's Woods, but thanks to you, I solved a mystery."

"No foolin'?"

"Yeah, something serious. It'll have an impact on a few young people's lives."

"What happened, sir?"

"It's a long story. I'll tell you about it sometime—over a cup of coffee."

"Yessir, sounds good, but right now, I gotta dee-dee outta here. My meetin's in less than an hour. I wanna catch some chow and head up ta Rockford."

It sounded like he had a good attitude. I hoped it would last. "Okay, hang in there, partner. Go to your meetings, and if you need anything, let me know."

"Yessir, thank ya."

He turned to go, but before clearing the doorway, he looked back.

"You're a good man, Captain. If ya want me ta go ta meetins, I will. I promise. You gave me my life back. Better not waste it no more. Right?" He flipped me a salute and left before I could respond.

THE END

About the Author

Wayne Zurl grew up on Long Island and retired after twenty years with the Suffolk County Police Department, one of the largest municipal law enforcement agencies in New York and the nation. For thirteen of those years he served as a section commander supervising investigators. He is a graduate of SUNY, Empire State College and served on active duty in the US Army during the Vietnam War and later in the reserves. Zurl left New York to live in the foothills of the Great Smoky Mountains of Tennessee with his wife, Barbara.

Zurl has won Eric Hoffer and Indie Book Awards, and was named a finalist for a Montaigne Medal and First Horizon Book Award. He has written four novels and more than twenty novelettes in the Sam Jenkins mystery series.

Author Links:

Author website: http://www.waynezurlbooks.net
Twitter: http://www.twitter.com/#!/waynezurl
Facebook: http://www.facebook.com/waynezurl